THE BOSS'S
SURPRISE SON

THE BOSS'S
SURPRISE SON

BY

TERESA CARPENTER

First published in Great Britain 2011
by Mills & Boon, an imprint of Harlequin (UK) Limited.
Large Print edition 2011
Harlequin (UK) Limited, Eton House,
18-24 Paradise Road, Richmond, Surrey TW9 1SR

© Teresa Carpenter 2011

ISBN: 978 0 263 22237 1

Harlequin (UK) policy is to use papers that are natural,
renewable and recyclable products and made from
wood grown in sustainable forests. The logging and
manufacturing process conform to the legal environmental
regulations of the country of origin.

Printed and bound in Great Britain
by CPI Antony Rowe, Chippenham, Wiltshire

For my beautiful niece Erika Beasley
and her handsome groom Aaron Miller

Congratulations, Mr and Mrs Miller

Welcome to the family, Aaron

CHAPTER ONE

RICK SULLIVAN left his office on the hunt for food. He'd been wrapped up in meetings with his department managers all morning going over end-of-year goals. They looked as if they would exceed projected sales. A good thing as he hoped to take Sullivans' Jewels into the international market next year to celebrate their centennial.

Not the best timing for his personal assistant to be out for knee surgery.

He noticed with relief that his new assistant Savannah Jones wasn't at her desk and moved over to flip the hourglass she kept on the corner. One end was white marble, the other black, and she'd asked him to place it black-side-up whenever he left the building. Apparently it was a pressing question when people saw his door was open.

When he got closer he saw he'd been both right and wrong. Ms. Jones wasn't *at* her desk, she was *under* it.

He slowly shook his head. He had two weaknesses: chocolate and his paternal grandmother. Both had the potential to get him in trouble, but where he could muster the discipline to say no to chocolate chip cookies, he'd never mastered the art of denying Gram's pleading blue eyes.

Which explained his current view of his new assistant's backside as she delved under her desk.

Temporary assistant, he reminded himself. His regular assistant, the highly efficient Miss Molly Green would be back in six months, two weeks, five days and—he glanced at his watch—three hours and forty-five minutes.

Damn right he was counting. And it was all Gram's fault. She'd convinced him to hire Ms.

Jones, a bit of fluff with little practical work experience and a penchant for chatter. Gram knew the Jones family, and when Rick blew through three assistants in the first three weeks of Molly's leave, Gram took advantage of his guilt and frustration to refer her friend and to insist he keep Ms. Jones on until Molly's return.

Though Ms. Jones's head burrowed out of view, he had no problem recognizing the half on display. Her bent position caused the gray fabric of her pants to pull taut, intimately framing the lush jut of her derriere.

Suddenly warm, he shrugged out of his jacket and without conscious thought walked around the side of her desk to get a better view.

His cheeks heated when he realized what he'd done. Annoyed at himself and her, he snapped, "Ms. Jones, what do you think you're doing?"

She started and a muffled "Ouch!" followed the sound of her head hitting the underside of the desk. "I'm…trying to…" She tugged on something out of sight, the motion causing her hips to wiggle enticingly. "...plug in my new electric stapler. But...the cord is...stuck."

More tugging, more wiggling, and he saw a bulky gray object shift on her desk.

Honestly, did he deserve this? It wasn't as if he expected his assistant to wait on him. He took care of his own coffee, dry cleaning and personal business. Were competent, efficient and prompt too much to ask for?

And okay, to be fair, in the four weeks she'd been here Ms. Jones had shown she understood instructions and could successfully proof her own work, which was better than the misfits he'd gone through in the first three weeks. But her methods were all over the place, much like her shifting hips.

"Ms. Jones, surely you could have called maintenance to handle this for you?" he asked impatiently.

"Gracious, I'm not going to call maintenance

just for a plug-in. The cord is just a little short, that's all. I'll be finished here in a moment. Did you need something?"

Wiggle, bend, wiggle.

Rick groaned as heat flared through him once again, and he almost strangled on his own breath.

Did he need something? Was she kidding? He'd be lucky to remember his own name at the moment. He should walk away, just end the torment. Yet, everything in him denied him the option of leaving her vulnerable to another man's approach. He glanced around sharply to make sure no male neared the vicinity. They were alone—both a blessing and a curse.

"Ms. Jones, I insist you remove yourself from under there this instant," he bit out.

"I've almost got it, but it's stuck. Can you push the cord through from that side?" she asked.

Anything to bring this scene to a close. He moved behind the desk and bent forward to shove the electric stapler closer to the opening for cords. Unfortunately the hole was full and the cord buckled up instead of dropping down.

He hesitated. He'd have to step between her legs to get the leverage he needed and somehow that seemed too intimate.

"Rick?"

"Just a blasted minute. You have too many cords in here." Manning up, he carefully placed his foot in the narrow opening between her shins and leaned over her to reach the tangle of cords. He shoved at the stubborn cord and his weight shifted, bringing his knee in contact with the soft cushion of her butt.

"Aha!" she exclaimed.

He nearly jumped out of his skin in his hurry to retreat to safety.

"That did it." Triumph rang in her voice.

He kept his gaze carefully plastered to her screen saver, a picture of her with her brother and sister, as she backed out and dusted off her hands.

"Thanks for the help." Her leaf-green eyes smiled as she ran a hand down the length of her mahogany ponytail to check it was smooth. "What can I do for you?"

His mind went blank. Why had he stopped at her desk?

"You can stay out from under your desk. We have maintenance on site for a reason. Next time use them," he ordered. Turning on his heel, he returned to his office.

His stomach growled as he sat behind his desk, reminding him of his original mission. He ignored it. He'd rather go hungry than wander out that door again.

The corner of Savannah Jones's lip curled upward in perplexed amusement as she watched her boss disappear into his office. What had that been about? He'd never even said what he wanted.

And for the first time the look in his piercing blue eyes sent a tingle zinging down her spine.

She shook it off and took her seat.

His high-handed attitude was nothing new. Nor was his gruffness—truly, the man could teach grim to the reaper—but his agitation and the fact he couldn't hold her gaze was.

Hmm. It was almost as if she'd made him nervous.

How interesting.

At six-one with thick dark hair, broad shoulders, narrow hips and piercing blue eyes Rick Sullivan had it all over Dr. McDreamy. And, oh, Savannah had it bad for Dr. McDreamy.

Wait. Wait. Wait. What was she thinking?

Rick made her tingle? She made him nervous? Neither emotion belonged in the workplace. And neither was good when there was no future for them except as colleagues.

She loved her new job, the challenge, the diversity, the responsibility. Executive assistant to the CEO of Sullivans' Jewels, a family-owned jewelry chain, was more than she'd ever dreamed of. More than she'd ever dared to hope for. Especially with her varied work history, from waitress to floral delivery to two years as a temp in corporate San Diego, she felt like she'd done it all.

She was determined to do a great job. She owed the Sullivans so much, especially Mrs. Sullivan, Rick's grandmother, not only for this opportunity but also for all they'd done for her sister. The Sullivan family donated two five-thousand-dollar scholarships a year to Paradise Pines students for their college education, renewable each year if the students maintained certain grade levels and continued to give back to the Paradise Pines community.

Savannah's sister, Claudia, had benefited from

their generosity for the past four years. She'd be graduating with honors later this year.

Savannah hadn't gone to college, and she'd been well into her twenties before she got her first job. Her high-school years had been spent caring for her mom. She'd been seventeen when the cancer eventually took her mom, and her dad had just disappeared into his work, leaving Savannah to raise her younger brother and sister.

So, yeah, she'd already done the family thing, but now Daniel was a cop in La Mesa with a beautiful wife and daughter and Claudia was about to graduate college. It was time for Savannah to think about her own career. She was done playing around, hopping from job to job. This might not be teaching, which she'd dreamed of doing long ago, but it was a career to be proud of, and she wasn't going to screw it up.

Even if Rick didn't have an aversion to a

workplace romance—and he'd made it more than clear he did—she had an aversion to workaholics. Been there. Done that.

Never again.

Rick worked, worked and worked some more. He was an expert at ignoring personal interaction on the job, to the point where he was considered positively antisocial by most of the staff.

He wasn't much of a talker, and, the Lord help her, she felt compelled to fill the quiet. So, while he read over reports and letters, she filled him in on all the office gossip. Nothing harmful, just birthdays, anniversaries, family events and such.

He probably didn't even hear her, though occasionally he'd hold up a finger for silence. So maybe he took in more than she thought.

Taking her seat, she noticed he'd flipped the hourglass black-side-up, which meant he'd been headed out of the office. She didn't know of any appointments, but he'd been tied up with his managers all day so he'd probably been heading for some lunch.

So why had he retreated to his office instead?

Hmm. Perhaps because she'd made him nervous?

With a grin she reached for the phone to order him a sandwich from a local deli that delivered.

The two of them might not have a future together, but it still felt good to send a man as hot and strong-willed as Rick Sullivan into an agitated retreat. Her self-esteem appreciated the boost.

After placing the order, she reached for her mirror and refreshed her lipstick, suddenly feeling very female and proud of it.

Being executive assistant to the president and CEO of Sullivans' Jewels demanded a professional appearance. Unfortunately, she'd spent too many years at home not worrying about her makeup or the need to tame her thick mass of hair.

Now a check in the morning and pop-up reminders in her email program kept her from becoming too frayed around the edges throughout the day.

Happily, she noted that there was nothing caught in her straight white teeth, which she considered one of her best features, thanks to Dr. Stevens and three years in braces, though she'd hated them when she was twelve, both Dr. Stevens and the braces.

Now she thanked the beauty gods for her straight teeth and plump lips, which she felt made up for her average features.

When the sandwich arrived, she knocked on Rick's door and got a finger wave to enter. He eyed her suspiciously as she crossed the room. Tickled by his reaction, she gave him a huge smile as she set the bag on his desk, causing his eyes to narrow even more.

"I thought you might be hungry."

"Thanks," he muttered.

"No problem," she said cheerfully.

She didn't linger but turned to leave and, because a girl had to find her fun where she could, added a little wiggle to her walk.

A strange sound, kind of a muffled groan, followed her exit. With a wicked grin she settled behind her desk suddenly energized to tackle the afternoon.

The next morning Savannah entered the conference room for her first monthly sales meeting juggling two boxes, a cup of coffee, her notebook and a pile of copies.

Of course Rick already sat at the head of the table. He glanced up at her with a pained look as she dropped her load on the table.

"You're late, Ms. Jones. What is all that?"

"Copies of the reports you requested plus doughnuts and a few bran muffins for the healthy-minded." She set her work and coffee aside and opened one of the boxes. "I hope that's okay. You forgot to tell me if you wanted bagels or doughnuts for the meeting, and I have a Donut Stop near my place so I just ran through there."

"I didn't forget anything," he corrected her. "This is a meeting, not a social event."

"Oh." Savannah blinked at him. No food at a morning meeting? The man was Scrooge. Seemed she couldn't do anything to please him. "I always thought it was a show of appreciation for valued employees." She set the box in the middle of the table toward the far end. "It'll be my treat today."

He scowled at that.

Undeterred—she'd learned while nursing her mother not to let someone else's mood bring her down—she opened the second box and pulled out napkins and plates, spacing them out over the table. And then she took the box to him, because he might be stiff, but she really did want to impress him and earn a permanent position in his company. "Would you like one?"

She expected him to refuse, but he surprised her by taking a chocolate cake doughnut and placing it on the plate she offered.

"Thank you."

"Doughnuts! Now you're talking." Rett Sullivan, Rick's twin and a co-owner of Sullivans' Jewels, along with their four brothers, walked through the door, snagging a cinnamon roll on the way to his seat next to Rick. "You should have done this years ago."

"You can thank Ms. Jones," Rick advised.

"Ms. Jones." Rett toasted her with his coffee mug. "Not only beautiful but sharp and generous, too. When I see you later, I'll have to thank you properly."

"I'm sure she got the message," Rick stated pointedly in a clear signal for his twin to desist.

In response, Rett winked at Savannah.

As identical twins, the two men obviously shared the same height, same build, same coloring. But Rett carried his weight leaner, meaner, his hair longer. Vice President of Design and Purchasing, Rett spurned what he described as the boring, restrictive suits Rick wore, stating they stifled his creativity. Instead, he chose matching dress pants and shirts in solid colors and rich fabrics. Today he wore a dark chocolate brown. The chain of his St. Christopher medal gleamed gold against his neck.

He was a charming flirt, easy to be with and easy to resist. They'd become friends when she asked him to teach her how to work with precious gems to design a gift for her sister's college graduation.

Rick's scowl landed on her again, and she quickly reached for the stack of copies and began putting one set at each seat around the table.

The doughnuts were a big hit as sales managers and associates began to fill the room. There was friendly chatter as everyone helped themselves. When she regained her seat, she slid a sideways glance at Rick. He was watching those in the room as if seeing them for the first time.

She wondered if that was a good thing. He began the meeting promptly at eight-thirty and kept to the agenda, moving smoothly from topic to topic while encouraging input from everyone at the table. He had her taking notes, but she noticed he also jotted down items when someone made a good point.

At the end of the meeting the room quickly emptied out, except for Rick. Savannah began clearing the debris.

"Ms. Jones?" He waited until she glanced up to meet his gaze. "What do you have going on with Rett?"

Savannah groaned internally. Just great. Because of Rett's playful comments Rick now had the wrong impression about them. She could tell him about the lessons; they weren't a secret. But she wasn't entirely sure he'd approve or believe she didn't have a thing for his brother. So she decided to prevaricate.

Avoiding his gaze, she dumped a load of trash and then picked up the wastebasket and brought it back to the table to finish the cleanup.

"I don't have anything with him today, but you wanted me to sit in on the meeting for the security upgrade and that's tomorrow."

He blinked, and then crossed his arms over his chest. "I *meant* are you seeing him?"

"I see him every day." She smiled and blinked, playing confused.

Should she just tell him? After all, it wasn't the office romance he feared. No, best not open a can of worms. The lessons were important to her and she didn't want to mess things up.

What if he wanted to see her work as proof? With two weeks of lessons under her belt she was thrilled at how well she was doing, but she was still new at the craft and by no means ready to go public with her efforts. Especially not to a professional jeweler.

"It sounded like he expected to see you later. As if you had a date," he stated baldly.

"Gracious no. That's just Rett." She waved a careless hand, her comment true, yet not an outright denial, a fact that didn't slip past Rick if his narrowed gaze was any indication. "He's a bit of a flirt, you know," she confided as if sharing a secret.

And then she just continued to smile and waited for him to move on.

And waited. He stood, hands in his pockets, staring at her.

"Or maybe I misunderstood," she said guilelessly. "Did you want me to find him and ask him something?"

"No. I—" He glanced at his watch, clearly still suspicious, but mindful of his schedule. "Never mind. Can you stop by the legal department on your way back to your desk? I want to know if we've received the signed contracts from Emerson for the international deal. We should have received them by now."

"Of course." Savannah dumped the last of the trash, glad to have avoided the confrontation. For now. He'd find out eventually. But she hoped to be indispensable by then.

Her lessons were important to her. But private. For years the classes she took at night and online had been her only freedom, her bid for independence from too much responsibility at home.

She still took courses that interested her or furthered her career. She just didn't talk about them much. Somehow, they'd always been too important to share. The knowledge, yes, but the classes, she kept to herself.

Nobody could steal the joy from her if they didn't know about it.

Rick turned to leave, and then paused. "The

doughnuts were a nice touch. Be sure to put in an expense voucher."

Savannah watched him go. Not so stiff after all.

Deciding he needed a break later that afternoon, Rick dropped by Rett's workshop to see if he wanted to go kayaking.

"Man that sounds so good." Rett didn't lift his head from the piece he was faceting. "But I have a client consult in twenty minutes. Can you wait an hour?"

"No. I only have about an hour. I'm going to go ahead and go. I really need to work off some tension," Rick said.

"Okay, we'll connect later in the week. Call me when you get back, so I don't send the Coast Guard out looking for you," Rett replied.

As he hopped into his kayak and began paddling against the waves, Rick realized he'd really needed the fresh air and exercise. Pitting himself against the ocean, using his mind and muscles to beat the elements gave him a sense of freedom he got nowhere else.

Unfortunately, the rhythmic lift, dip and pull of paddling, first one side and then the other, left room for thoughts of Savannah to invade his mind. Darn it. Too often thoughts of her occupied him when he should be concentrating on business.

The idea of her spending private time with Rett nagged at him. And not just because of Rick's policy against interoffice relationships— Rett followed his own rules in that regard and was much less strict in his personal interaction with colleagues.

But Savannah was Rick's. Oh, not romantically, but still, he realized he didn't want to share her with anybody.

He dug in deeper, pulled back harder, causing water to roll over the sides of the shallow boat.

Okay, he'd noticed her soft curves and her great legs. Of course he'd noticed; he was a man after all. But he had no business noticing. She was his administrative assistant, not his girlfriend.

His inappropriate thoughts served as a reminder of why he never mixed business with pleasure. It was a bad practice. It definitely led to trouble and, for him, it had no future.

His muscles burned and the chill, salt-laden air felt good against his sweaty brow.

Marriage wasn't for him. In his experience love was always followed by pain. Better to keep his relationships light and put his energies into the business.

As for Savannah, he wished her gone, not hanging out with Rett.

Turning the kayak, Rick firmly put thoughts of Savannah's body, dating and marriage aside and headed back to shore. He had a business to tend to.

CHAPTER TWO

RICK had stepped out for lunch the next afternoon when a pretty redhead toting a baby carrier stopped by Savannah's desk.

"Hi, I'm Rick's sister-in-law, Jesse," the
woman introduced herself. "His brother Brock's
wife. Is he in?"

"I'm sorry, no. I'm his new assistant, Savannah.
Can I help you with something?" she offered.

"Right, Savannah." The woman offered her
hand with a genuine smile. "Gram speaks very
highly of you. She mentioned something about
you working with Rick."

"Mrs. Sullivan is a doll," Savannah enthused.
"I really appreciate her putting in a good word
for me with Rick. I'm very excited to have this
opportunity."

A fussy cry came from the carrier, and Jesse grimaced at Savannah before cooing at her baby. Once the fussing quieted, she looked up again.

"I have an appointment with Rett to discuss a gift for Gram for her eighty-fifth birthday. The guys are throwing a big surprise party, so they want it to be something spectacular."

"She'll love that. When is her birthday? I'd love to get her a little something to show my appreciation."

"Oh it's not for another few months." Jesse rolled her eyes at herself. "I know, I'm way anal, but I like to start early. And we want a really spectacular gift so it's only fair to give Rett plenty of time to work. But Troy is awake and alert now and wants attention. I was hoping Rick would take him for a few minutes while I consult with Rett."

"Oh, well…" Watching a baby, even his own nephew, didn't sound like a Rick activity, but

Jesse must know her brother-in-law better than Savannah did. "How long do you expect to be?"

"Only about twenty minutes. That's all Rett could squeeze in today, but we wanted to get started and at least discuss what we want to do." She bounced the carrier when another cry sounded. "Never mind. I know Rett won't mind—he loves the kids. We just won't get as much done as we'd hoped."

Savannah glanced at the hourglass; most of the sand had already fallen to the bottom half. Rick rarely took a full hour for lunch. "He should be back soon. If you like, you can leave Troy here with me and I'll watch him until Rick gets back."

"Really? That's so nice of you." Relief brightened Jesse's features. "He's fed and newly changed, so he shouldn't be any trouble." She set the carrier on Savannah's desk. "Thank you so much."

"No problem. How old is he?" Savannah asked.

"Five months." Jesse handed over Troy's diaper bag. "I'll be as quick as I can." With a wave, she rushed off.

"We'll be here, won't we, baby?" Savannah talked to Troy, smiling gently. Babies liked her. She figured they had her number. She was mush in their tiny hands and they knew it.

She spent a few minutes getting acquainted before lifting the little boy from the carrier. She cuddled him and then settled him in her lap, bouncing him lightly while she went back to the numbers.

That worked for ten full seconds. Troy's tiny fingers wrinkled the paper. She just got that away from him and he knocked her pen to the floor. Rescuing that as well, she turned him around and sat him on the desk facing her.

"You're a busy boy. Are you trying to be like your uncle Rick and work, work, work?"

Troy grinned at her and then promptly burped up.

"Oh, baby." She reached into his bag and pulled out a cloth to clean him up. "That's better, but let's see if we can get you rinsed off."

She lifted Troy to her shoulder before setting the diaper bag in the carrier and carrying both into Rick's office. He had a private bathroom. She set the carrier in his empty in-basket and took Troy into the bathroom to clean him up.

Rick strolled into his office after lunch and froze in shock just inside the door. A baby carrier sat in his in-basket. With a frown he glanced back at Savannah's desk. It was empty.

What was going on? He moved to his desk, but the carrier was empty, too.

What was Savannah up to now? Babysitting no doubt. People here already had her pegged as an easy mark. Well, he'd put a stop to this. There was a limit to his patience. And babies topped the list. His brothers popped them out on a regular basis; well, their wives did, and more power to them.

Rick preferred to keep his distance. Not that he was nervous or anything, it was just that babies were complicated. You had to hold them just so, bounce them a certain way, make sure they didn't touch things. Feed them, change them, burp them. Yes, definitely complicated.

A baby's cry shot tension straight up his spine. There was no ignoring that wail of displeasure. A moment later Savannah walked out of his bathroom with a baby boy in her arms.

"So there *is* a baby here," he said, looking from her to the boy in her arms, ready to take her to task for wasting time. Wait, the kid looked familiar. "Does it belong to one of my brothers?"

"Yes, *he* is your nephew, Troy." She bounced the boy gently. "Do you think five months is too young for an apprenticeship?"

"Oh, yeah, we'll just put a nanny on staff."
He opened his top drawer and tossed his wallet
inside. "Where are Brock and Jesse?"

"Jesse is downstairs going over preliminary
designs for your grandmother's birthday gift
with Rett." She shifted the baby. "Do you want
to hold him?"

"No." He took an involuntary step back.

Savannah lifted both brows at his reaction.
"No? With your large family I'd think you'd be
used to kids."

"Yeah, well, kids aren't really my thing."

"Really?" His answer shocked Savannah.
"How can you resist such a charmer?" She
turned Troy to face him. "He's adorable. And
babies are so easy to reach, all you have to do
is smile and coo."

To show him, she smiled at the five-month-
old.

Troy shyly smiled back.

"See?" She glanced up at Rick and got caught in his watchful gaze.

"Pull yourself together Ms. Jones. I never coo," he said firmly.

"Well, that's a shame." The baby squealed and bobbed in her arms. She felt bad for Rick, that his icy reserve prevented him from finding joy in his infant nephew. "Maybe you should try it sometime. Babies love unconditionally, you know. It's kind of a win-win situation."

He cocked a dark brow, reminding her silently that she was speaking to the boss.

"Right. What was I thinking?" She back-pedaled a bit. She needed to leave the room before she said something she'd regret. She knew she talked too much. Her sister, Claudia, said it was Savannah's biggest weakness and her biggest strength; she tended to say too much, but she also had the power to put people at ease.

Rick tolerated her chatter fairly well, though he rarely spoke himself. Rather he observed and directed, often without saying a word. He orchestrated her comings and goings with the crook or staying motion of a finger. For the first week she'd felt as though she danced to the tune of the puppet master. Now she appreciated the efficiency of their system.

She just wished he could connect with his nephew, who was so lovable and accepting. Maybe if he held Troy, he'd be swayed by the baby's sweetness.

When the phone rang, she grabbed her chance.

"I should get that. Here, take Troy for just a minute." She plopped the boy into Rick's arms and reached for the phone, carefully keeping an eye on the pair as she spoke.

He skewered her with a glare. Though he seemed uncertain, he instinctively cradled Troy against his shoulder, looking more as if he held a fragile piece of spun glass than a living, breathing child.

Why did a single man holding a baby always look so sexy?

Of course, Rick always looked good. Her first week of work she'd had a serious talk with herself about keeping her eyes off the boss.

Yeah, right. The man was serious eye candy so that didn't work.

But she wanted this job and that did. So yeah, her ambition helped her keep her hormones in check. That and Rick's workaholic habits and stern demeanor.

Today none of that seemed to matter. Not when he looked so vulnerable, strong yet gentle, with the baby cuddled in his arms.

Not wanting to press her luck, she wrapped up the call. "Sorry about that." Savannah took a step toward Rick. "I'll just take him back—oh, baby!"

Troy burped up, all down the front of himself. And Rick.

"Sh—" Rick broke off a curse. His reflexes

in holding the baby out and away had not been quite fast enough to save himself from a nasty dousing, including on his shiny black loafers.

Troy's brow puckered up, and Savannah grabbed the wet cloth from his seat and rushed forward to clean him up before he started to cry.

"It's okay, sweet thing, you're fine, you're good." Once she had the baby all mopped up, she turned to Rick and swiped at his white shirt. After she got the worst of the mess off the front of him, she lifted her gaze and met his blue eyes, which were much closer than she had anticipated, and were focused on her with a mixture of irritation and awareness.

"Sorry, that's the best I can do," she said, her voice huskier than normal.

"Thank you," he said, his voice calm and controlled, his gaze holding hers. "I think you should take him until Jesse returns."

"Of course." She hastily stepped forward, almost tripping over her own feet as her nerves tingled. A ring sounded through the open door and she paused. "Oh, there's the phone on my desk."

"Let it go to voice mail," Rick ordered. "I need you to take Troy while I change my shirt." Without waiting for her response, he passed the baby into her care.

The phone on her desk stopped, and his began to ring.

Even as he picked up the receiver the other hand went to the top button of his shirt. He made quick work of both the call and stripping to the waist.

Savannah swallowed hard, tempted by the sight of bronze skin and hard muscles. A taut, lean torso supported broad shoulders and narrowed to lean hips. The ocean-kayaking he did with his twin showed in the defined muscles of his arms.

"Savannah." Her name was a buzz in her ears until he thrust the phone into her hand. "Take down the details of this conference call for me. I'll be back in a minute."

"Of course." She watched his strong back disappear into his private bathroom before turning her attention to the task. Easily juggling baby and receiver she jotted down the information from the manager of the San Francisco branch.

When Rick returned a few minutes later retucked and retied she pushed the memo slip into his hand and, carrying Troy, began to back toward the door.

"I'll just go find Jesse." She made her escape.

At the door she snuck a quick peek back. Rick sat behind his desk. Once again at work, once again in control.

The sight sent a longing through her she couldn't explain. And couldn't afford. Not when she still tingled from the tempting view of his hot body.

She loved her new job; the work interested and challenged her. And she'd learned a lot.

But suddenly she looked forward to Rick's upcoming trip to Europe. Thank goodness for the international deal he'd closed.

After the moment of heated awareness between them, having a full continent and an ocean dividing them for a week seemed like a really good idea.

Troy smirked at Rick over Savannah's shoulder as if happy to have her to himself. That drew a reluctant grin out of Rick. The boy was a true Sullivan.

Savannah was another matter. Rick had never known the irrepressible Ms. Jones to be so skittish.

Why he found her quick retreat so fascinating he couldn't say. Maybe he just liked seeing her flustered. She deserved it after tossing the baby at him and then standing so close that the sweet scent of her hair teased him even over the stink of baby burp, sending a spark of aware-ness streaming through his blood.

The shock of watching the gold flecks sparkle in her green eyes triggered an inappropriate physical response inside him he had no inten-tion of acting on.

The last thing Rick wanted or needed were lascivious thoughts about his assistant. What a train wreck that would be.

Better to be annoyed than aroused by her.

The best thing would be if she quit. Hmm, he mulled the idea over. He saw two problems with that option. Gram would blame him, citing his promise, and Savannah wouldn't be so easy to get rid of. She actually seemed to like her job.

She might talk too much, but she didn't jump if he said a sharp word, unlike the temps before her. And she didn't squeak at the long hours unless there was a conflict with a family event.

He understood family obligation. One of six brothers, Rick had a large, close-knit family that liked to get together on a regular basis. He participated because of Gram and because it was expected, but he often felt isolated even when he was part of the crowd. It'd been that way since he was a kid.

He loved his brothers, but he'd never found it easy to share, except with Rett, of course. That had always been enough for him. Especially after his broken engagement in college.

Losing people hurt. In his opinion, loneliness was a small price to pay for peace.

"Hey, Rick." Jesse strolled in, her baby in her arms. "I really appreciate you and Savannah helping with Troy. Rett and I came up with some great ideas for Gram."

"I'm glad." They exchanged a few pleasantries as she efficiently strapped Troy into his carrier.

"I'm sorry to have to run off, but I have to get Allie from preschool," Jesse explained.

"No problem. I'll walk you out." Rick saw

Jesse into the elevator across the hall from his and Savannah's offices. "See you later."

"Oh, I almost forgot." Jesse stopped the doors from closing. "Do you know your grandfather's birthday? We need to know his birthstone for Gram's gift."

Rick frowned as he raked his mind. "No. Sometime in the summer, but I don't remember when."

"I have it," Savannah said, and he turned to her in surprise. "It's in Molly's history file. There are biographies on all the past presidents, including dates of birth and dates of death." Her fingers clicked at the keys of her computer as she talked. "Charles Sullivan was born July 23. Do you need the year?"

"No. This is wonderful." Jesse beamed. "You've saved me. I thought I was going to have to pump Gram without tipping her off about the party. Can you let Rett know?"

"Sure. I'll send it to his email."

"Thanks. And thanks again for watching Tr—" The elevator door cut off Jesse's words.

Blessed silence descended on the office.

Rick sighed and met Savannah's gaze to see an understanding gleam of amusement.

"Yeah," Savannah agreed as she went back to the papers in front of her. "You love to see them. And you love to see them go."

"Huh." She'd nailed it on the head.

It felt strange to have her read him so well. Strange for anyone to make the effort with him. People tended to avoid rather than interact with him. Generally that suited him fine, but the moment of connection warmed him in an odd way. Turning back to his office, he rubbed absently at his chest.

She still talked too much.

The next afternoon the ringing of the phone summoned Savannah as she approached her cubicle after a late lunch. Rushing to answer, she expected the call to be business-related but was surprised to find her sister, Claudia, on the other end.

A very excited Claudia.

"Oh, my God, Savannah. I love you. I love Mrs. Sullivan. I love Rick Sullivan. I love *all* the Sullivans."

"Hold on, slow down." Still catching her breath, Savannah struggled to understand her sister's chatter. "What are you talking about? What has Rick done?"

"I just heard that because I'm going back to Paradise Pines after I graduate, they're going to give me a bonus scholarship to help me get settled as I start my new job. That means—"

"Wait a minute." Savannah sat down, setting her purse on the desk. "You're telling me the Sullivans gave you *more* money?"

"Yes. Savannah, I'll be able to get my own apartment, and a new computer. And a new wardrobe. I need to thank a Sullivan. I need to thank them all. Mrs. Sullivan didn't answer her phone so I thought of Rick. Is he in?"

"I don't understand." Savannah felt thick-headed, but this was so huge. "You mean even though you'll be out of school, they're giving you *another* five thousand?"

"Yes!" Claudia's excitement reached squeal proportions, dimmed only slightly by the distance of the phone. "This is so amazing! Can you believe it?"

Yeah, Savannah could, when she got past the shock enough to take it all in. One of the things she admired most about the Sullivans—including Rick, the whole doughnut incident notwithstanding—was their generosity.

"You deserve it. You've worked really hard these last four years," she told Claudia.

"I'm overwhelmed. Thank you."

"Don't thank me. Thank Rick." Just when she had him pegged as all work and no play, Rick did this. Something so thoughtful and sweet it showed what a truly decent man he was. And she knew he was involved because Mrs. Sullivan had told her he had the final say over the scholarships.

"I do thank you. You've always been there for me. And of course, Rick, too. Is he there?"

Savannah glanced up at his closed door. "He's on a conference call. But I'll tell him you called."

"Oh, okay. I know you're busy so I won't keep you. Promise you'll give Rick a big kiss from me. Love you lots. Bye."

"Claudia!" Savannah protested.

But her sister hung up, leaving Savannah with the image of kissing Rick. A visual she really didn't need. After the incident with Troy yesterday it was easy, way too easy, to imagine how he'd taste, how he'd feel against her.

She'd never known a man like him, so physically fit, so stern in demeanor. All male, he made the men she'd dated seem like boys in comparison. Not that there'd been that many boys. Her high-school years had been spent caring for her mother instead of flirting.

Savannah never quite recaptured those flirty, experimental years. And, ever since, she'd felt one step behind in the game of love.

Unfortunately, Rick really made her wonder what she'd been missing.

A few minutes after Rick's conference call wrapped up a knock sounded at his door. He looked up as Savannah peeked around the edge.

"Good, you're free," she said, stepping into his office. Her fitted skirt showed her legs to advantage as she made her way toward her usual chair in front of his desk.

Even then she didn't stop. She kept coming, clear around the desk.

At the determined look in her eyes, he surged to his feet. When she leaned toward him, he leaned away. But she kept on coming, lifting onto her toes to touch her lips to his cheek. Instead of pulling away, he bent over her, breathing in the soft scent of honeysuckle.

Now why hadn't he guessed she'd start the afternoon with a kiss?

"That's from Claudia," she said, now intent on avoiding his gaze as she rose on her toes again and her lips caressed his other cheek. "And that's from me."

Her hair brushed his cheek as she moved back. He clenched his fist to keep from pulling her closer.

"You Sullivans have been incredibly good to her. She's over the top about the bonus money for returning to Paradise Pines."

Ahh. Rick resisted the urge to shift restlessly as he resumed his seat. "The scholarships are my grandmother's purview."

"And *she* told me you always participate in the final decision," she countered.

Caught, he shrugged. "Paradise Pines needs

young professionals. We're just doing what's good for the community."

"Claudia will be great for the community and she'd be returning to Paradise without the incentive, but thank you." She hesitated, as if she might say something more. Or kiss him again. Instead, she nodded and turned to return to her desk.

Today she was calm, collected, with no sign of the flustered woman from yesterday.

Perfect. Cool and distant were good.

He could use a little indifference himself. Watching her long-legged retreat on red-hot heels, he fought the urge to loosen his tie, the airy room feeling suddenly overly warm.

He should be happy to be back on a professional footing, but for some reason he wasn't.

"Savannah."

"Yes." She stopped at the door to look back at him, her leaf-green gaze wary.

Right. No point in embarrassing them both.

Which meant no more inappropriate thoughts of Savannah, short skirts and his desktop…

He pulled a legal pad toward himself. "I'm glad your sister is happy."

CHAPTER THREE

"Your design is lovely."

The next Monday after work, Savannah stood in Rett's pristine workshop for their regularly scheduled lesson, watching as he held her sketch, turning it this way and that to view it from all angles.

"The setting will look great in gold, intertwined but independent with the classic emerald anchoring the middle. The symmetry is aesthetically beautiful. Your sister is going to love this piece," he told her.

"Thank you." Satisfaction and excitement made her giddy. But anxiety kept her grounded. She intended the pendant and earrings as a gift for Claudia's graduation, so Savannah needed it to be perfect. "You don't think it's too ambitious?"

He hit her with amused blue eyes. "You passed ambitious when you decided to design the pieces in the first place, so don't get wimpy on me now."

"I'm not." His approval of her design only made her more determined to finish the project. "But my skills are pretty new. I played around with beading when I was younger but this is the first time I've worked with precious gems."

"Relax, you're a natural. Your designs are busy enough to have interest but simple enough to have classic appeal. Plus I'll be doing the actual gem work."

"I know and I really appreciate it." She smiled sheepishly at him; it was strange relying on someone else's opinion of her work. His praise felt good, but at the same time it was hard being judged. She focused on the positive. "Someday I want to learn to facet, too."

"Why don't you take it one step at a time? Here, let me show you something." He walked across his workroom and unlocked a drawer under the counter running the length of the wall. He pulled out a small, clear box and brought it over to her.

"Open it." He placed the box in her hands.

Through the clear container she saw a brilliant green. Curious, she flipped the lid. Inside nestled a set of emerald earrings. Round cuts in an intricate swirl of yellow gold.

"This is my design!" Her gaze flew up to meet his.

He nodded. "You left your drawing on the counter last week."

"You made my design into real jewelry?" she demanded, both surprised and proud.

"That is what we do here at Sullivans' Jewels," he reminded her with a smile.

"Yeah, but I'm an amateur."

"Yes, it is, and yes, you are," a deep voice said

from the doorway. Rick wove his way around the worktables in the middle of the workshop to reach them. "You're working with novices now?" he asked his brother in disbelief.

"We all start somewhere. But don't worry. She's good. See for yourself." Rett handed Rick the earrings. Turning back to Savannah he assured her, "This is a great design, but you may want to wait to make a decision on which design you use until after we've had a few more lessons."

"Good idea." Chewing her bottom lip, she watched Rick as he inspected her work. Talk about being judged. Rett, at least, was an artist, but Rick was all business, he'd look at her work from an entirely different perspective. She told herself she respected his knowledge and his taste.

And still she held her breath.

"These are nice, very elegant. I'm impressed," Rick said. He pinned Savannah with a pointed stare. "So this is what you two have been up to."

Ignoring his comment, she focused on his approval: Rick's words of praise made her feel like a diamond, valuable and brilliant.

"Why are you down here, Rick?" Rett asked, taking the earrings back.

"I received some news. The Emerson Group is pulling out of our international deal."

"What the heck?" Rett exclaimed, his hands going to his hips in an automatic, challenging stance.

She understood his confusion. She'd heard how long and hard they'd worked on the international anniversary event and suddenly it was null and void?

"What happened?" Rett asked. "Jack Emerson seemed excited by the alliance. I can't believe he changed his mind."

"Jack suffered a heart attack last week. That's why we hadn't received the final documents.

His board of directors invoked the rescission clause," Rick said heavily.

"Oh, my God." Savannah had talked to Emerson a couple of times; she'd liked the older man, finding his bluntness and honesty refreshing. "Is he okay?"

"He had triple bypass surgery. He's home and doing fine, but he has some recovery ahead of him."

"Man, I'm sorry." Rett shook his head, showing his support with a clap on Rick's shoulder. "You've worked so hard on this deal."

Savannah knew months had gone into Rick's plans to lease international sites for Sullivans' Jewels. In the last ten years, he'd taken the family-owned company national by opening stores in Beverly Hills, San Francisco, Las Vegas, Dallas, Chicago and New York. To celebrate the company's one-hundredth anniversary, he intended to take the company international. That plan might be in jeopardy now.

"Too hard to give up now," Rick answered grimly. "I've gone through the notes on our alternative choices. I like Crosse International as a close second. Albert Crosse has agreed to meet with me next Tuesday. That gives us a week to regroup and put together a new plan. Savannah, I need you to pull the notes from our earlier negotiations. I want a list of our points of agreement and dispute."

"Of course. Rick, you know I'll work over the weekend if necessary to be ready for the meeting."

"Thanks." Even distracted he sent her a brief glance of appreciation. "But we'll be traveling over the weekend. Our meeting with Crosse is in London. Since I had the trip planned, he's offered us a suite at his London hotel. You'll need to cancel the other reservations."

"We?" she exclaimed.

"Yes, I'll need you to go with me."

"London." Stunned, Savannah sank onto a

nearby stool, pictures of Big Ben, Buckingham Palace and Westminster Abbey flowing through her mind.

"Savannah?" Rick brought her back to the moment.

Everything was moving so quickly she had to stop and clarify. "You want me to come with you to England?"

"I'll need you there, yes." He leaned back against the work counter, his gaze running over her. Not that he saw her; his mind was clearly on business strategy.

"I can handle the change in reservations, but I'm not sure I can get on the same flight as you." The thought of traveling with him gave Savannah mixed feelings. A trip to Europe thrilled her. Being alone with him really didn't.

"Then change my flight." Rick glanced at his watch. "Can you stay? I want you working on the Crosse deal full-time. If we're going to meet our deadline of opening the first international store by November next year, this deal has to close by the end of December." Leading the way out of the workshop, he outlined their timeline. "That gives us two weeks to finalize the negotiations and site the European stores."

"I'll get started right away," she said.

Savannah couldn't believe her luck. Being involved in these new negotiations really gave her a chance to prove herself in the job. And it would look really good on her résumé. Not to mention the exciting trip to England.

Okay so she'd be sharing a suite with Rick. But with so much on the line, surely she could control her hormones for a week?

Thursday night Rick sat brooding in his office. He'd had one ambition when he took over as CEO of Sullivans' Jewels: to make the family business so strong it would never be vulnerable again.

As it had been under his father's control.

The store almost went under after his parents' death. Gram held it together with grit and sheer determination. Rick and his brothers had helped where they could. He and Rett had only been ten, but they'd gone into the store with her on weekends. And when they got older they put in more time. He'd helped Gram while Rett hung out in the design workshop.

And when Gram announced her retirement and handed the company over to him, he'd made the hard choice to put family first. He'd sacrificed his engagement in order to stay in San Diego and take over Sullivans' Jewels.

Maybe when they celebrated the company's one-hundredth anniversary in their first international store, he'd feel he'd finally succeeded where good old Dad had failed.

By rescinding their offer, Emerson had cost Rick six months toward the completion of his goal. Now, in order to meet his December deadline, he needed to hit the floor running.

Savannah had really come through for him these past few days. With her help he'd restructured the package for Crosse International, including acceptable concessions for being second choice. When they touched down in England, they'd take Crosse by siege.

A knock sounded at the open door as Savannah entered the room. He watched as she strolled toward him across the office floor.

"Here are the profit and loss statements for the past two years. Accounting is still working on the amended projections for this year. I set up an appointment with the CFO for tomorrow morning." She handed him the files then sat and crossed her legs, waiting for a response.

With determined professionalism he looked away from the tempting sight of her navy skirt inching over her knees onto her thighs.

After reviewing the documents, he tossed the file on his desk. The action startled Savannah, catching her in the middle of a yawn. Sometime during the day she'd removed her jacket, but otherwise she looked as fresh and serene as when she'd walked through the door this morning.

He winced when a glance at the clock revealed that had been close to thirteen hours ago.

The overhead light cast fiery highlights in her dark red hair, drawing his attention. She wore the mahogany mass up on her head but this late in the day escaping tendrils cascaded over her neck and brow. Maybe not so fresh after all, but sexy.

Way too sexy. And touchable.

He definitely had no business wanting to touch her.

He needed to give the woman a dress code, he thought with an inward groan, one that included oversized jackets and buttoned-up shirts. Looking at all the toned, creamy-white skin revealed by the light gold, sleeveless, scoop-necked blouse, he knew he needed to change the course of his thoughts or risk embarrassing himself.

They'd been working together since before seven this morning and it was after eight at night now. A repeat of the past two days. What he needed, what they both needed, was a break.

As if on cue, Rett strolled through the door. "You guys still working? I thought you said you had the proposal pretty much wrapped."

Rick leaned back in his chair.

"We do. The attorney has it. We'll get his comments in the morning and go through it one last time. I was just going to suggest we call it a night and start out fresh tomorrow." That was good, that should end the torment of the day.

Except Rett had other ideas. "Hey, you have a fifteen-hour flight on Saturday. You'll be begging for something to do to fill the time. Save your review for then and give Savannah tomorrow off."

"Wait a minute," Rick protested.

"Come on." Rett dropped into the second visitor's chair. "I bet she's already put in over forty hours. With all the overtime she probably hasn't even had a chance to pack. Have you?" He directed the question to Savannah.

"What?" Her eyes grew big as the attention centered on her. "Oh, well actually—"

"See." Rett waved a triumphant hand. "Think about it," he tossed at Rick. "In the meantime, why don't I call and make reservations for the three of us for dinner. You both deserve a decent break."

"I really should head home." With a weary sigh Savannah rose to her feet, drawing Rick's attention once again to her blouse, and the way sunshine clung to her breasts. Much as he strived for professional detachment, yellow had just become his new favorite color.

"No, join us," Rett insisted. "You've worked hard. Let us treat you to dinner."

She hesitated for a moment and then smiled.

"Okay, you only have to ask me twice. Why don't I meet you at the restaurant? Then I can just leave from there."

They finalized plans and Rick insisted on walking her to her car. Then he followed her to his favorite steak house, silently cursing his brother's interference.

Rick disliked mixing business with pleasure, and dinner with Savannah definitely blurred the edges of personal and professional. Her performance this week had surprised him; he could admit that. And despite the occasional distraction of her stunning legs or the sweet scent of her shampoo, they'd accomplished an amazing amount of work. She'd stayed calm and often anticipated him, providing reports and stats before he could ask.

Dinner should be innocent enough with Rett along.

Yeah, strictly business. In fact, he'd use dinner

to discuss options on where they should open the first international store.

Unfortunately just as he reached the restaurant Rett called to say he couldn't make it after all. Rick couldn't help but curse.

Savannah waited just inside the door, buttoned into her jacket, her hair once again neat and tidy.

"Rett blew us off for a date, so I guess that leaves just you and me," Rick said bluntly.

She bit her lip, drawing his attention to the plump, pink perfection of her mouth. "Maybe I should just go home. It's been a long day."

He should grab the offer, but the weariness in her sea-green eyes got to him. "No, stay. You have to eat and this will be better than some fast food you pick up on the way home." Not waiting for an answer, he settled his hand in the small of her back and indicated to the maître d' they needed a table for two.

She quickly stepped ahead of him, leaving him with a view of her gently swaying hips as he followed her to their table. Telling himself the hunger clawing at his gut was for food, he ordered a rib eye.

"I want something I can sink my teeth into," he declared with a smile.

Rick's words caused a fluttering in Savannah's insides. She'd like to dismiss the response as a symptom of hunger, but unfortunately she was too self-aware for the flimsy excuse. Really, she should have headed straight home and avoided any chance of an intimate dinner with Rick. But the thought of having to cook after the long day—days—she'd put in held as little or less appeal than a plastic drive-through meal. And she'd thought she'd be safe with Rett along, too.

The waiter delivered their drink order. Rick placed both arms on the table and leaned forward. "I've pretty much narrowed the choice of location for the first store to London or Paris. I know you put together a list of properties earlier this week. What are your impressions?"

Okay, she knew the key to maintaining an emotional distance from him hinged on concentrating on work, and she appreciated being asked for her opinion. But she couldn't take any more today. Her brain couldn't hold another fact.

She inhaled a bracing breath, and then met his gaze. "Can we talk about something besides business?"

For a moment shock stole his voice. "What?" he managed to croak.

"My brain is fried. No more shop talk." She outlined her rules in clear, concise terms.

Rick stared at her, clearly speechless. Yet after a moment he relaxed back into his seat and opened his hands, palms out to her. "Sure. We'll talk about whatever you want."

"Try to hold back your enthusiasm," she said with a wry smile as she reached for a roll. Tearing it in half, she put the remaining half back in the bread basket.

Totally at ease in his habitual black suit and white shirt, Rick exuded elegance and class, putting most of the other men in the room to shame. The broad stretch of his shoulders and confident tilt of his dark head added to his sense of presence.

He looked good, really good. He always did, but tonight she found it hard to look away. She should be leery, especially when his gaze revealed he liked looking at her, too, but she didn't have the energy. Instead she enjoyed the delicious tingle of excitement zipping along her nerves.

A sensation common sense promptly squashed.

She didn't want the situation to change. She valued this job too much to risk it on the unsteady influence of romance.

"Okay." Rick picked up the half roll, took a bite. "Where'd you learn to speak French?"

"High school. I took it instead of Spanish. And

then I took an advanced class in night school. After the class ended a bunch of us would get together for dinner at a French restaurant once a month and only speak French. It helped to cement the language. Especially if others in the restaurant joined in." She popped the last bite of roll in her mouth then licked a smudge of butter from her finger. "I sign up for classes and seminars all the time."

"Seminars?" he asked, his interest caught. "What topics interest you?"

Lifting one shoulder in a half shrug, she said, "All kinds of things, child development, business courses, design, some self-help classes where you learn how to end clutter in your life or build up your psyche with daily affirmations. That kind of thing."

"Ah." He nodded in understanding. "Sounds… boring."

His honesty surprised a laugh from her. "Some of it, yes. Some are ridiculous. Some are definitely more helpful than others. I just enjoy getting out, learning something new."

"Like jewelry design and faceting?" he said.

"Exactly."

The waiter arrived with their salads and to top up their water.

"Share something ridiculous," Rick demanded as soon as the waiter left.

Ridiculous? That shouldn't be hard. The man had a master's degree in Business Administration; he'd probably find most of what she went for ridiculous. Actually, she knew just the thing to tickle his fancy.

"In Strengthening Your Relationships, to get into your partner's point of view, you're supposed to strip completely naked, lie down on the bed and imagine yourself as a man."

"I *am* a man." No hesitation. No apology.

Oh, yeah. As if she needed to be reminded of his male factor.

"*You* would be imagining yourself as a woman."

His dark eyebrows spiked up. "That *is* ridiculous. Who thinks these things up?"

"Doctors, therapists." She speared a bite of lettuce, dipped it in her dressing. "The point is to see, to feel, to react from the aspect of your mate."

"Sensitivity training." The corner of his sensual mouth curled down, indicating what he thought of the idea. "You almost make it sound interesting."

"Thanks. I think," she said, defiant, though in truth his comment pleased her. She liked the thought of engaging his interest. But she wasn't sure she didn't agree with his obvious disdain of the topic. In fact, her imagination was working overtime, putting *naked*, *bed* and *man* together, and not just any man, but Rick.

Heat rose in her cheeks, and she reached for her ice water to cool off.

Rick's gaze narrowed then became intense as he slowly chewed and swallowed. "Why relationship seminars? You haven't mentioned a man in your life."

She wished she had a name to give him, that in truth she had a man in her life. If she were involved, Rick would be easier to resist. But there hadn't been a man in her life in close to seven months. And then it had been more of a friendship than anything else.

She demanded a lot when it came to love. She wanted what her younger brother had found with his wife, Kathy, what her mother and father had had before her mother died and her father buried himself in work. A loving partner to spend her life with.

"I'm ready for a new relationship," she admitted slowly.

"With a man who pretends he's a woman?"

"No." Amused, she shook her finger at him. "You're trying to mess with me, but it's not going to work. The sensitivity training was just a class. And I admit I got more out of the seminar on clutter control." She swirled her glass on the table. "Have you tried to patch things up with Diana?"

He'd broken up with the woman just after Savannah had started at Sullivans' Jewels. Diana had called several times over the past couple of weeks. Rick had taken the calls but they'd been very brief.

The waiter appeared, holding steaming plates of fragrant food. He stepped aside so the busboy could take the salad dishes, Rick's empty, hers half-eaten.

"Careful, the plates are hot," the waiter said as he set the dishes down, asked if they had everything they needed and then discreetly disappeared.

Rick frowned as he picked up his knife and fork. "It's over. We had some good times, but she was looking to change the rules, so it was time to end it."

"Of course, you have relationship rules." She shook her head as she took a bite of her fish. "I'm curious, what do you have against marriage? Most of your brothers are happily married. From what I've heard your parents and grandparents were happily married, yet you seem to be dead-set against it. Why?"

"I'm not against marriage," he denied. "I wish my brothers and their beautiful wives all the best. It's just not for me."

"Why not?" she pressed, trying to understand his position. "I'm focused on my career right now, but in the future I want a family, a partner and a couple of kids. Don't you see that for yourself someday?"

"I have a huge family, lots of nieces and nephews. I don't need kids of my own. My work gives me more satisfaction than any relationship I've ever been in."

Although Rick was not normally a man to be pitied, Savannah felt sorry for the lonely future he outlined.

"I love my job. Thirteen-hour days notwith-standing." She sent him a telling glance through thick lashes, and then smiled. "But I can't see it being enough for me. I need family in my life."

He nodded, his features expressionless as he focused on cutting his steak. "So you'd choose family over work?"

"Probably." Time to turn the tables. "What about you?"

"I love my job, too." Laughter brightening his blue eyes, he toasted her. "Thirteen-hour days notwith-standing."

Appreciating his comeback, she raised her glass and clicked rims with him. Still, his evasion challenged her. He didn't often open up like this—okay he *never* opened up like this—and she perversely welcomed the chance to get to know more about him.

Perversely because she knew better than to open herself to him.

"I meant, don't you want love in your life?" she asked curiously.

"No." He didn't even hesitate. "I'm not getting married," he reminded her. "Love isn't worth the pain."

He'd been hurt. The sharpness of his tone revealed a depth of emotion he kept carefully buried. He'd lost his parents when he was so young. She knew how tough that was, knew how every subsequent loss to the heart compounded the pain, leaving you feeling raw and exposed. Those were not emotions that would sit easily with Rick.

It saddened her to see such a strong man give up.

"I'm sorry for your pain, but love hurts because it's important." She gently covered his hand with her own. "It doesn't mean you have to give up on having a family of your own."

His openness closed down in a blink as he pulled his hand free of her touch and disappeared behind a facade of indifference.

"It's not a loss if it's not what you want."

Or if you told yourself you didn't want it so the hurting stopped. Kind of what she'd done with her dream of going to college.

"You're right." Common sense returned on a wave of self-preservation. Why let his attitude bother her when she had self-deceptions of her own? Suddenly uncomfortable with the topic, she sought a change. "Who started this conversation anyway?"

"You did," he reminded her as he pushed his plate aside. "You said you wanted to settle down someday and have a family."

"Right. Well that's a long way in the future." Nodding to the waiter's offer of coffee, she dismissed the serious conversation with a careless wave of her hand. "I'm not looking for anything permanent right now." She met his gaze over her mug. "So maybe I need to know more about those rules you were talking about."

CHAPTER FOUR

"I'M THINKING of going back to school for a teacher's degree," Savannah announced to her sister the next afternoon. When Claudia had learned Savannah was traveling to London, she'd insisted on a shopping trip to update Savannah's wardrobe.

Claudia rounded the rack of dresses in a stylish boutique at the mall and gave Savannah a once-over and then, totally serious, nodded her head and said, "I think you'd make a really good teacher."

"Really?" Savannah couldn't hide her wistfulness. "You're not just saying that because you know it's what I want to hear?"

"Dude, you know that's not me. I don't do pretty little lies. And in this case I don't have to. You're smart, patient and creative, all great traits for a teacher. I think you should go for it."

"You don't feel I'm too old to bother now?" Savannah asked.

"Phff. There are people of all ages at State, but if it bothers you, try online classes. These days you can practically get your degree without ever going to the classroom." Claudia absently pushed a few hangers along the rack. "But isn't this kind of sudden? What brought this idea on?"

"I've always wanted to go to college, but I didn't really know what I wanted to study. Something Rick said last night really started me thinking. Teaching feels right. But it's been so long since I was in school."

"What did he say?" Of course, Claudia snagged on the Rick element.

"I was telling him about some of the seminars I've attended at dinner last night, and he said I made something ridiculous sound interesting."

"At dinner you say?" Claudia wiggled her dark brows.

"Oh, stop. It was a reward for putting in a long day."

"It sounds like you had a good time."

"Yes. I mean, no. It wasn't like that. And believe me, I put my foot in my mouth before I was through." She went on to tell her sister how she'd tried to change the subject when it got too uncomfortable.

"You asked him about his dating rules?" Claudia smirked at Savannah over a rack of cocktail dresses. "How brave of you."

"The conversation was getting heavy." Savannah shook her head at the red mini dress Claudia held up. The color would clash with the red in her hair. "I was trying to lighten things up."

"Right." Claudia eyed the red dress, shrugged and draped it over her arm. The color would be stunning with her own coffee-brown hair, green eyes and pale skin.

"Ohh, look at this." Claudia held up a black dress and the breath caught in the back of Savannah's throat. It was fitted from the hips up, with wide bands of material that wrapped the dress, crisscrossing each other over the breasts and then flaring out to create short, off-the-shoulder sleeves. A full, flirty skirt would swirl several inches above the knee.

"It's beautiful, but I can't. This is a business trip. I'll have no occasion to wear a cocktail dress."

"You never know. It's always good to have a little black dress along on a trip just in case. And this material will travel really well. Come on, at least try it on."

Giving in to temptation, Savannah disappeared into the fitting room. Of course, she loved the dress. It fitted like a dream, making her feel pretty and special.

She stepped out to show Claudia.

"Oh my." Her sister circled Savannah, practically purring. "You *have* to buy it. If you don't, I'll buy it for you, and I can't afford it."

Savannah did want it. "It has no sleeves. It'll be too cold to wear in England."

"My roommate is from New York. She has a beautiful black wool overcoat you can borrow."

"I can't borrow your roommate's coat."

"Sure you can. She never wears it unless she's going home. Come on, Savannah, you know you want it."

Savannah grinned. "Yeah, I do. But probably not for England."

"Please. Wear this to dinner and Rick will forget all about his rules."

"Oh, no. No." She shook her finger at her sister. "He can keep his rules. I just didn't want him thinking I was looking to get married and leave Sullivans', or that I was desperate for a man."

Claudia laughed as she went back to shopping. "Instead he probably thinks you were hitting on him."

"Oh, my God." Appalled, Savannah rounded the rack and caught Claudia's arm. "Is that what it sounded like to you?"

"Calm down." Claudia pried Savannah's fingers loose. "I was just kidding."

"No, you're right." Weak as the events of last night replayed through her head, Savannah sank into a chair outside the fitting room. "I was trying for light and sophisticated, but it sounded like a proposition." She mimicked a stab to the heart. "Just kill me now."

"Such drama. That's more me than you." Claudia squeezed Savannah's shoulder. "Sister mine, I love you, but we both know the flirting gene skipped you."

Tragic, but true. Still Savannah shook her head. "He doesn't know that."

"Okay, so what did he say? What are these famous rules?"

"He didn't answer. The waiter came with the check and the moment was lost. And that was the end of dinner."

"He just left?" The notion clearly outraged her younger sister, who'd been wrapping men around her little finger since infancy. Even their father responded to Claudia. Of course she was the shining image of their mother, which helped.

"No. Rick is too much of a gentleman to do that. He walked me to my car. Oh, gosh, and then told me I could have today off and he'd see me at the airport. Oh, this is bad. First the kiss and now I've propositioned him. I'll probably get home and find a message telling me I've been traded with Tammy from accounting."

"Whoa, whoa, whoa! Stop right there." Claudia dropped to the floor to sit cross-legged in front of Savannah. "You never mentioned a kiss. Spill! I want all the details."

Heat rose in a tide from Savannah's chest to her hairline. "It's *your* fault. *You* told me to thank him for the extra money from the scholarship."

"You actually *kissed* him?" Claudia demanded. "On the *mouth?*"

Savannah blinked at her. "Of course not, on the cheek, but you're missing the point here."

"Right, right. I see the problem. In the last two days you've kissed him *and* hit on him."

Savannah groaned. "That's it. I've cost myself the perfect job. And a trip to Europe."

"He's really got you twisted up. I've never seen you so flustered over a man."

"He's not a man. He's my boss."

"Oh, sweetie," Claudia admonished her. "He's *all* man and if you're trying to ignore that, no wonder you're in trouble."

"You're not helping," Savannah said.

"Helping? Right, you want to know if he realized you were hitting on him."

Savannah gritted her teeth.

"Hmm." Claudia tapped her lip while she thought. "Did he revert back to business?"

"No." Savannah perked up, seeing where her sister was going. Work would be an instinctive barrier for Rick to throw between them if he felt she'd gotten too familiar. "He asked how the plans were going for his grandmother's birthday. That's good, right?"

"Yeah, I think you're safe. He'd have played the work card if he wanted to shut you down. He probably just didn't want to talk about his love life."

"There's no love in his relationships." With a relieved breath Savannah pushed to her feet, helped Claudia to hers. "That's what the rules are about."

"Another reason for him not to answer you. Nobody that knows you could see you in a loveless relationship."

* * *

Savannah's plan as she strapped herself into her business-class seat on the airplane was to act as if it were business as usual when Rick arrived. No talk of rules or relationships. Or anything else. She'd guard her tongue if she had to bite it off.

This was one time when his lack of talking would be welcome.

Where was he anyway? She leaned over the aisle seat to glance up the companionway but there was no sign of her stalwart boss. She'd been surprised when he wasn't waiting for her in the departure area, but as the boarding passengers began to dwindle, she began to worry.

There shouldn't be any traffic at this time of night. They were taking the red-eye to New York and would catch an international flight out of JFK in the morning.

Frowning, she looked at her watch. Oh, God, what if he didn't show? Did she fly or get off the plane?

Just as she reached to ring the flight attendant to ask if he'd checked in, he strolled through the door.

And—*oh my.*

Rick in a business suit was controlled elegance, a man who knew what he wanted and how to get it. Rick in jeans and a navy T-shirt was big and broad and just a little rough around the edges, a man who took what he wanted and enjoyed the challenge.

She couldn't take her eyes off him the whole time he stowed his gear and took his seat.

When he met her stare with his take-no-prisoners blue eyes, she blurted, "I was about to flip a coin to see if I should fly without you or get off the plane."

He didn't apologize, simply said, "Rett drove me to the airport."

"Oh. And he was late?"

"He wouldn't think so." Rick grimly stated what sounded like an age-old argument between the brothers. He tucked a newspaper in the seat back in front of him. "Rett and I have a difference of opinion about how much lead time you need when you're flying."

"Why do you let him drive you then?"

"As he pointed out, I haven't missed a plane yet."

"Well, this wasn't the one to start with," she informed him, still a little on edge at the close call, a feeling that nudged up a few notches when the plane door closed.

"Settle down, Ms. Jones. I'm here safe and sound."

"Let's hope you stay that way," she muttered under her breath.

"What does that mean?" Of course he'd heard her.

"Nothing," she evaded, her attention focused out the window at the city lights as the plane began to roll.

Now Rick had arrived, there was nothing to

distract her from the fact she'd soon be taking to the air in a very heavy object. Biting on her lower lip, she reminded herself thousands of people flew across the country every day.

Suddenly a strong, warm hand closed over hers on the armrest, stilling her tapping fingers.

She followed the reverse angle from hand to hair-dusted forearm, to muscular biceps, to strong neck, stubborn chin and eyes narrowed in suspicion.

"Don't tell me you're a nervous flyer," he accused.

"I don't know." She pulled her hand free. "This is my first time flying. I'm sure I'll be fine, but right at the moment, yes, I'm a little nervous."

"Huh." The suspicion backed down to mild irritation. "Don't you have a Valium or something you can take?"

Now that was just rude.

"I don't need to be medicated. I need a distraction." She almost changed her mind about that as the plane picked up speed rushing down the runway and she felt the wheels lift.

Okay, oblivion may not be such a bad thing.

She cleared her throat and concentrated on the conversation. "Don't worry. I'm not going to jump into your lap or anything."

"That's good to know," he said as he dug her nails out of his arm.

"Sorry." She smiled weakly, and, reclaiming her hand, she sought her own distraction in her carry-on. The first thing she pulled out was a plastic zip bag of home-baked chocolate chip cookies—nothing distracted or soothed as well as chocolate—and the second thing was the newest novel by one of her favorite authors. Rick had his paper so she didn't need to feel bad about reading her book. And once she started reading, she'd get caught up in the characters, mystery and romance.

After tucking her tote back under the seat in

front of her, she dug out a chocolate chip cookie. Taking a healthy bite, she settled back in her seat and sighed, feeling the tension leave her body as she chewed.

Next to her she heard Rick sniff the air. From the corner of her eye she saw him slowly turn in her direction.

"Are those chocolate chip cookies?"

"Yes. But you wouldn't hold my hand so you can't have any."

"A tad cranky tonight, aren't you?"

"It's the nerves. I want to fix it, but I just have to get through it." Because she wasn't mean, she turned the open bag of cookies toward him. "Peace offering?"

He took a cookie. "You still can't jump in my lap."

She grinned. "Spoilsport."

"But I suppose I can sacrifice a hand occasionally if you feel the need."

Her insides warmed at the offer, evidence

the grouch did have a heart. But, oh, not good. Warm feelings for Rick were too much of a distraction. She'd better stick to the chocolate.

"Thanks." She held up a second cookie. "But I'm feeling better already."

"Good. Because it's a long flight. Do you think you'll be able to sleep?" He licked a smear of chocolate off his finger, a sensuous move she followed with her eyes.

This relaxed Rick fascinated her, which made him very dangerous indeed.

"Savannah?"

"Huh?"

"Do you think you'll sleep?" he repeated.

"Oh. Eventually. I can sleep anywhere." She zipped the bag of cookies and tucked it in the seat back in front of her. "How about you?"

"I'll doze."

"Maybe *you* need the Valium."

He laughed. A hearty sound she realized she'd not heard from him before.

How sad, she'd worked closely with the man for close to two months and had never heard him laugh. She immediately wanted to make him laugh again. He really needed lightness in his life, but this was another thing she couldn't fix, not without putting herself on the line emotionally, something she couldn't risk. And it didn't even have to do with the job.

She couldn't risk opening her heart to a man obsessed with work.

The loneliness, the lack of support, the disappointments—she wouldn't, couldn't go through that again.

So, instead of continuing the conversation and coaxing another laugh from him, she said, "Do you mind if I read for a while? I think it'll relax me."

The laughter faded from his eyes and he shook his head. "Go ahead. Will it bother you if I work?"

"Not at all."

With a curious sense of letdown, she lowered her tray table and opened the hardback to page one. Luckily, the characters soon drew her into the action and before long she was caught up. Flying, Rick, the sound of him typing all faded to the background as she outright giggled at what she was reading.

Rick couldn't sleep. Not with the soft scent of honeysuckle tickling his senses, a constant reminder of the woman occupying his companion seat.

At least she finally slept. She'd read for a while, and had a great time of it, too, if the musical sound of her laughter was any indication.

He glanced at the book, wondering again what she found so amusing. Since she appeared dead to the world, he reached for the book and read the front blurb—and then the first page.

An enjoyable hour had passed when he next

looked at his watch. Stifling a yawn, he returned the book to where she'd had it stowed.

To stretch his legs he walked to the restroom at the far end of the plane. When he got back, he stood looking down on Savannah.

She sat half-turned toward him, a hand tucked under her cheek, so young, so sweet, so lovely. Cinnamon curls caressed creamy-white skin while dark lashes fanned over her cheeks. She shifted in her sleep and a pretty pink tongue swept over full, bare lips leaving them damp and as inviting as the smudge of chocolate above the corner of her mouth.

Fatigue must be getting to him because he wanted to lick her, first to eat the chocolate beckoning to him and next to taste the plump line of her lips, to sink inside and share the treat with her.

What on earth?

He rubbed his eyes. Pull it together, man.

To escape further temptation he slid into his

seat and stared at the boring weave of the blue-and-gray fabric of the seat in front of him.

What had possessed him to bring her on this trip? He'd have been better off with someone from legal, someone fifty and comfortably thick.

Okay, so she'd been a great help prepping for the upcoming meeting, but she was still more optimistic than organized, totally unpredictable and distressingly unafraid of anything. A little healthy trepidation would make her so much easier to control.

She had yet to meet a stranger. The woman made friends wherever she went.

When was the last time a woman had made him laugh? He couldn't remember. More importantly, when had he become such a staid old man? So he cared about the business, cared about providing for his family. Did that have to mean he gave up on fun, gave up chasing all the enjoyable pursuits life had to offer?

Of course not. He determined to broaden his horizons when he got back. Spend more time with his brothers, read for pleasure and find a new woman friend.

Right. He closed his eyes and hoped by the time he got home—with the international deal sealed—the idea would hold more appeal.

The plane suddenly shook and then dropped, startling Rick out of a light doze. Instinctively, he grabbed the armrest before he even opened his eyes. His fingers closed around flesh and bone rather than hard plastic.

Savannah. Concerned, he glanced her way. She slept on but a slight furrow creased the fine porcelain of her brow. He pulled his hand back, granting her use of the armrest. She immediately became restless and the frown deepened.

He covered her hand again, twining his fingers with hers and she stilled and settled back into slumber.

She was as soft as he'd known she would be. Not that he allowed himself thoughts of her.

Another shake, a lift and then a sharp drop. Someone screamed and Savannah came awake with a start. She blinked at him.

"What happened?" Husky from sleep, her voice stroked along fine nerves, causing the hair on the back of his neck to tingle in aroused awareness.

"Just a little turbulence."

"So I didn't dream a scream or that the plane was shaking?"

"Ladies and gentlemen." A calm voice came over the public-announcement system. "We are experiencing some heavy turbulence and the pilot has turned on the seat-belt light. Please remain buckled in your seats until he turns off the seat-belt light. Thank you."

Savannah's trembling fingers tightened on his. "Are we going to be okay?"

"I've heard no plane has ever gone down because of turbulence."

"Really?"

"That's what I've heard," he said reassuringly.

"Right. Oh, gosh." They were thrown back in their seats as the aircraft dipped and swayed.

"It shouldn't last long." He sought to relieve her distress. "The pilot will try to get either above or below the problem area."

"That would be good." Her agitation showed in the rapid rise and fall of her breasts. "That would be really good."

She fell silent as the plane continued to rock and roll. And he watched her to make sure she didn't hyperventilate. White knuckles defined the clasp of their hands, but neither fought to ease the hold one had on the other. He didn't expect the plane to crash, but he wouldn't deny he took comfort from the connection.

The flight evened out for about ten minutes,

just long enough for everyone to begin to relax, when the shaking began again.

The drastic drop in altitude got to him, but the distressed whimper from the seat next to him was like a fist to the gut. Acting on impulse, he lifted the armrest between them and pulled her into his arms.

She clung to him and, lifting tearful eyes to his, pleaded, "Can't you make it stop?"

In that moment he'd give anything to fix it, to bring the laughter back to her eyes. He couldn't stop the turbulence, but perhaps he could take her mind off it.

"You have some chocolate on your face."

She blinked. "Huh?"

"Right here." He lowered his head and licked the corner of her mouth, sweeping the chocolate up with a flick of his tongue.

CHAPTER FIVE

SAVANNAH felt as if the plane had done a loop-the-loop, turning her world upside down. She went still as Rick's mouth teased her, his tongue swirling over her skin.

Snug in the warm clasp of his arms, her existence narrowed to just the two of them. Strong and solid, he made her feel safe, protected. The scent of him, familiar and all male, surrounded her. And she wanted more of him; she wanted that mobile mouth on hers. But he continued to flick and nibble at the edge of her lips, close but not close enough.

With a low growl of need she turned her head and found his mouth with hers. Yum.

As if he'd been waiting for just that, he opened his mouth over hers and took control of the kiss, plundering her mouth with deft finesse, stealing her ability to think.

Sensation took over. Chocolate, hot and sweet, exploded over her tastebuds. She hummed with approval and met his tongue in a passionate tango of thrust and retreat. He lifted her, half pulling her into his lap, only her seat belt hampering him from completing the action.

Oh, better. Looping her arms around his neck, she threaded her fingers through his short, mink-soft hair, holding him to her, drawing his essence in and giving herself back.

"Ladies and gentlemen, the pilot has turned off the seat-belt sign. You are now free to move about the cabin."

The announcement washed over them like a bucket of cold water. They broke apart, and Savannah buried her face against Rick's chest.

The world came rushing back—the plane, other passengers, the near-death experience.

For a while none of it had mattered; now it all did.

She bit back a groan as her brain reengaged and she realized where she was. In the boss's arms. This was not good, not good at all. It helped only slightly that Rick's heartbeat matched the racing pace of her own.

How to extricate herself?

"Restroom." She fumbled for her seat belt. "I've got to go." Once she found the release, she bolted to her feet and escaped down the aisle. Luckily, there was a line of people waiting. Maybe it would last until they reached New York.

Five people and two hours to kill? Not even she was that optimistic. Which meant she'd have to sit next to him with the blood still speeding way too fast through her system. Thank goodness her jacket hid the aroused state of her nipples because if it was cold in here, she didn't feel it.

All too soon she was sitting in her seat again, her jacket wrapped around her, staring at the gray hair of the man seated in front of her while Rick focused his attention on the ceiling.

Not comfortable with being uncomfortable, she said, "Thank you. I was scared and you… helped me. It was very kind of you."

He made a choking sound. "Don't mention it. Please."

"I wasn't propositioning you."

He turned his head slowly and pinned her with an intense stare. "What are you going on about now?"

"The other night at dinner when I asked about your dating rules. I wasn't propositioning you." She cleared her throat and dropped her eyes. "In case you think I've been throwing myself at you."

"I didn't." He went back to his contemplation of the ceiling. "I don't."

Instead of reassuring Savannah, his simple

dismissal struck a contrary chord. It wasn't as if there was no chemistry between them. The last few minutes had proved that conclusively.

"Well, all right then." She let silence fall between them, telling herself she should be glad to have that worry gone. But she couldn't help herself. "Why not?"

Her pique must have sounded in her voice because he sighed.

"I know when I'm being propositioned. And flirting isn't your style. You're too straightforward."

"Then why didn't you tell me the rules?"

"Because there isn't a hope in hell you'd ever abide by them."

"I don't know how you can know that," she retorted, stung.

"The rules are about establishing personal boundaries to prevent expectations of a deeper relationship from forming. You have personal relationships with everyone."

"Not everyone."

"Everyone," he insisted. "Including the mail boy."

"He goes to State, which is where my sister attends college. So yeah, we've chatted a few times."

"What's his girlfriend's name?"

"Amber."

"I rest my case."

"That only proves I'm a good listener."

"I've worked with Molly for twelve years and I don't even know her daughter's name."

"Oh. Well." His confession stunned her so she had no argument for him. "What was your point again?"

"That my rules aren't meant for you."

For a moment it sounded as if he meant that his rules didn't apply to her, and a wild rush of pleasure bloomed in her. She quickly squashed it, first because she knew how he intended what he'd said, and second because he wasn't for her.

Anyone who worked with someone for twelve years and didn't know something as intimate as her daughter's name was too impersonal for Savannah.

She could never be with someone who believed that work was more important than people. And that described Rick to a T.

"You're right," she conceded. "Your rules aren't for me."

To Savannah's relief the trip concluded without further incident and they arrived in London exhausted but ready for the upcoming meeting. After spending fifteen hours practically joined at the thigh with Rick, she was ready to retreat to her own room.

"Beautiful hotel," she commented on the way to the elevator, admiring the large leather furnishings and dark woods amidst marble and crystal. "I see now why you were drawn to Crosse International."

"What do you mean?" he asked as they boarded the elevator.

"The ambience. A modern feel in a traditional setting. You know, kind of a comfortable chic."

Rick simply nodded and she wondered if he was even listening. Except for business, he'd kept conversation between them to a minimum ever since the embrace on the flight to New York.

Savannah closed her eyes and sighed at the thought of stretching out in a bed. She was *so* ready for some alone time.

"It reminds me of the store back home," she muttered.

"What does?" Rick held the elevator door for her to exit.

"The hotel. Oh, we're right here." Savannah had never been so happy to reach a destination. She slid her key card into the slot. "See you in the morning."

As she closed her bedroom door, she almost

had herself convinced she was pleased by his impersonal attitude.

Almost.

So call her crazy. She wanted to have her cake and to eat it, too. Working so closely with Rick these last few days had twisted her emotions in a knot. His drive and dedication challenged her while his intelligence and dry sense of humor made the long hours speed by.

Not to mention every little touch tested her ability to remain unaffected, from the accidental brush of skin against skin to the warmth of his breath on her cheek as they bent over the proposed contract.

All in all, her feelings for him weren't as easy to ignore as she'd hoped. And the awareness growing between them buzzed like static in the air.

But if he could pretend indifference to the passionate kiss they'd shared, so could she.

Right.

* * *

Savannah slept like the dead, waking only when her alarm went off. She showered and dressed in her navy suit with the gold scoop-neck blouse. She wanted to look good and the outfit made her feel confident and professional.

When she entered the parlor suite connecting her room to Rick's, she found him already sitting at the dining table reading the paper. He'd ordered coffee along with an array of muffins, yogurt and fruit.

"Good morning," he greeted her, his glance up from the paper slightly leery as if he feared what she might say, or perhaps it was that she might start chattering.

He needn't worry; she liked to ease her way into the day. After helping herself to coffee and fruit, she took a discarded section of his paper and enjoyed the quiet and the view.

Having the meeting with Crosse in the hotel was convenient, allowing them to leave their room at ten to ten and simply ride the elevator down. But that was the end of her peaceful morning.

The meeting was the crash and burn they had narrowly missed the day before, or it would be if Savannah didn't act fast.

True to form, Rick masterfully presented the numbers and projections, but his confidence and all-business approach came across as arrogant. Albert Crosse, a fit man in his early sixties, flanked by his two sons, listened but seemed restless. And the more Rick pushed, the further apart the two got.

She tried to catch Rick's eye more than once, but he ignored her, so she took matters into her own hands.

"Mr. Crosse." She spoke into a tense silence. "I was wondering which property you would suggest for the joint venture?"

Rick shot her a repressive glance. "Ms. Jones, this isn't the time—"

"Please." Crosse waved Rick off. "I don't

mind, though you must remember to call me Albert."

"Of course, Albert."

Short and compact, Crosse exuded a charm and charisma that exceeded his stature. His presence demanded attention, and, though his sons were present, it was obvious Crosse ruled.

He leaned forward and clasped his hands on the table. "Actually, I believe this property would be spot-on for your purposes. This location runs at seventy-five percent or more capacity for most of the year. We've already converted first-level offices into retail space and have leases with a full-service day spa and a coffeehouse. There are two more spaces available."

Perfect. This was better than she'd hoped for when she'd taken the discussion off topic. A field trip would change the current dynamic and, she hoped, get the negotiations flowing again.

"Gracious, right here in the hotel? Can we go see the space? After the long flight yesterday and sitting most of the morning I'm a bit stiff and would welcome a chance to stretch my legs."

"Ms. Jones—"

Savannah turned so only Rick could see her and silently mouthed, "We're losing him." Aloud, she said, "I know we have an appointment with the property manager later, but I'm sure Albert will be an excellent guide."

"Splendid idea. It would be my pleasure." Crosse talked right over Rick's objections. "I'll have the property manager meet us there. I was scheduled to inspect the conversions today, but agreed to take this meeting instead."

"Will we have an opportunity to finish our meeting?" Rick asked as everyone stood.

"I have some thinking to do tonight," Crosse advised him stiffly. "I'll have my assistant call you with a time for tomorrow."

When they reached the lobby, Crosse stopped to talk briefly with his sons who were taking this opportunity to break away.

"What do you think you're doing?" Rick demanded, pulling Savannah aside.

"We were losing him." She moved to watch the Crosses so Albert couldn't walk up on their conversation. "We needed a distraction."

"That's ludicrous." He dismissed her claim. "This is a solid proposition."

"Yes, but he was already sold on the numbers—you sold him on those before. And then you chose to go with someone else. Now he's wondering what's to keep you from jumping again if a better deal comes along."

"Sullivans' Jewels has a solid reputation. And we made concessions."

"On paper." How could such a brilliant man be so dense? "You are an exceptional business strategist, but in this instance you need to read the man. It's a matter of loyalty, of pride. Think how you'd feel if the situation were reversed."

He frowned, but she'd caught his attention. Seeing Crosse's conversation was breaking up, she stepped closer to Rick and lowered her voice. "You said I relate to everyone. Well, trust me on this. Let him know he can trust you." Hooking her arm through his, she turned him toward Crosse. "And when we tour the space, don't bring up the deal. Business is fine but stay away from anything personal. Connect with him on another level."

She felt him stiffen before pulling away. "I think I know how to conduct myself with a business colleague."

"Of course." She stepped away, feeling awkward. What had she been thinking linking arms with him like that? She was his assistant, not his girlfriend. "Sorry. Go do your magic."

Rick hated to admit it, but Savannah was right.

A good thing for her, because if she'd blown

this deal she'd be gone, promise to Gram or no promise.

He'd known Crosse was antsy. Yet, instead of stopping to think it through and adapt to the situation, he'd let the man's stoic response cause him to push harder.

Rick didn't like being in this position. He was used to being the one making decisions, not the one waiting for the nod.

But more importantly, Savannah had hit the biggest issue on the mark. If the situation were reversed he'd want more than facts and figures thrown at him. Despite any concessions tossed his way, he'd want to know Sullivans' Jewels was more than a second choice. After all, they weren't just talking about the lease of space; they were talking about partnering brands to broaden their demographics.

The insight made him stop and question himself. Had his goal become more important than the process? Was he rushing his decisions to meet his self-imposed deadline? If that were the case, he needed to stop now and reassess.

He kept his mind open to the possibilities as they toured the space with Crosse. His first impression was of the size. It was smaller than any of their other stores. But the prime location, right on the lobby, and accessibility to the old vault one story down were strong factors in its favor.

Because he agreed with the strategy, he heeded Savannah's advice to avoid talk of the proposal except for renovations and contractors in general because Crosse brought them up. By the time they completed the tour, including visits to the spa and coffee store, he'd made a decision. The process and the goal were both right-on.

"Albert, thank you for your time." He shook Crosse's hand. "They say all things happen for a reason and in this case I need to agree. I originally went with Emerson because I thought their traditional image was a closer match for Sullivans' Jewels. After staying here and talking with you and your sons, I see I was wrong.

"We're both family-owned and family-run companies. And our styles are very similar— 'comfortable chic,' Savannah called it last night."

With nothing to lose, Rick spoke from the heart. "I know you're hesitant about going forward with the project, but I hope you decide in our favor. The fact is we fit very well indeed. And I'm excited about the prospect of working together. I think I can learn a lot from you."

"Hmm." Albert stood with his arms crossed, nodding. They were totally mixed signals: one said he was closed off, the other that he was listening. He turned to Savannah, who had drifted to the background during the tour. She'd asked a few questions but had mostly followed quietly as the men wandered and talked.

"Beautiful lady, what am I to make of this

bloke? Upstairs he is cold and calculating, so serious with the numbers. But down here he comes alive, and shows passion and heart. Which is the true man?" Albert asked.

Savannah smiled. "Both, of course. Upstairs he's looking forward to what could be. He knows his business and the numbers tell of the possibilities. Here—" she spread her arms to indicate the vacant space they'd returned to "—it becomes real. He can see his store, feel it, breathe it. And, yes, he's serious about his business. He is the heart of Sullivans' Jewels."

Crosse angled his head at Rick. "Beautiful and loyal. You are lucky, Rick, to have someone who believes in you so strongly."

"Yes." Truthfully her response had surprised Rick. He knew he'd been tough on her from the beginning, yet she'd nailed him with that comment. He found it more than a little disconcerting.

"I have much to think about," Albert stated.

"I'll have my assistant contact you regarding a time when we can meet tomorrow."

"Is it all right if we view the other London properties as time allows?" Rick requested.

"I see no harm in that," Crosse agreed.

Rick inclined his head. "We'll be waiting for your call."

Happy to be out of the snow and cold, Savannah crawled into the back of a taxi, scooting over to allow room for Rick. As she settled into the worn leather seat, her relief at being out of the weather shattered as her hand came to rest against Rick's muscular thigh on the bench seat.

Immediately the heat of his body warmed the backs of her icy fingers. For the thousandth time that day she rued forgetting her gloves at home.

Rick's head whipped around. It took every ounce of poise she possessed to meet the awareness in his blue gaze with a semblance of calm professionalism.

Unfair. Unfair. What a cosmic joke if she had to fight him as well as herself to keep their relationship on a business level.

She racked her mind for something to distract his attention from her. A street sign caught her attention. "Buckingham Palace. It must be close, can we drive by?"

He looked over his shoulder at her with lifted brows, but he leaned forward and spoke to the driver.

"Thank you." She'd seen some lovely sights as they made their way through town to the Crosse properties—St. Paul's Cathedral, the Millennium Bridge. Seen but not experienced.

"I know we're here on business, but please tell me we'll get some free time to actually visit some of these beautiful sights."

She saw him looking at her out of the corner of his eye. "I suppose you deserve something for your interference today," Rick conceded. "You were right about Crosse. He needed reassurance. You saw that and quite possibly saved the deal."

"I hope so." She shifted so she faced him. Watched as he lifted a hand to smother a yawn. The muscles in his throat worked and her mouth watered. "I liked Crosse."

"He liked you, too." That was the second time in two days he'd said a man liked her. Knowing she shouldn't go there, she couldn't prevent the question from popping out.

"Do you?" she asked.

"Yes. I was being honest with him. I really do think I can learn from him."

"No," she corrected, "do you like *me?*"

His profile froze before he slowly turned and shot her a harassed glare. "What do you mean?"

"Never mind, it doesn't matter." What was she thinking asking such a personal question? Other than that somehow his answer mattered a great deal to her.

"What are you talking about?" he asked, genuine puzzlement in his tone. "Everyone likes you."

"So you seem to think." Stop this now, she pleaded with herself. But she didn't care about everyone; she cared about him. "But what about *you?* I know you think I talk too much."

"You do," he said with casual ease. "But I'm getting used to it. I even learn things, like 'comfortable chic.'"

She grinned. His announcement had both surprised and pleased her. "I noticed how you used that." And how he'd skipped over her question.

"I meant what I said. You changed the direction of the meeting today. Thank you."

"I'm sure you would have noticed before it was too late."

"Don't start lying to me now, Savannah. I like to think I would have caught on eventually, but you don't think so or you wouldn't have interrupted."

"Well, you were overexcited—"

He laughed. "Now that's something I've never been accused of before."

"It's not a bad thing. And you're entitled. Oh look, it's the guards with the bearskin hats. And, oh, the palace."

The view was out Rick's window and she had to lean forward and toward him to catch sight of the grand palace. Even in her excitement she noticed how good he smelled, clean with a hint of spice. It made her want to snuggle close, and she'd already practically climbed in his lap in order to see better.

"Savannah." He ground out the throaty protest.

And, of course, he was right. The one time under extreme conditions on the plane could be excused; twice and it was getting to be a bad habit.

"Sorry." She eased back into her own space and lost all sight of the palace. "Driver, please stop," she called.

"What are you doing?" Rick demanded.

"I'm getting out. I can't come to London and not see the palace. I'll find my own way back."

"It's freezing out there. Literally."

"I'll be fine. I may even find a shop to buy some gloves."

She reached for her purse and when she looked up she saw an odd flash of emotion cross Rick's face. The vulnerability in his hooded gaze stunned her, brought a lump to her throat. For a moment, the strong, confident man looked lonely.

"You should come with me," she heard herself say. "We can find a pub and have some fish and chips."

He hesitated, then surprised her by nodding. "Sure. I could eat."

CHAPTER SIX

As a distraction, Buckingham Palace ranked right up there with chocolate and shopping in Savannah's estimation. In fact, having a studly companion as she strolled the block fronting the majestic building and grounds didn't suck either.

The snow-drenched grounds were well-lit, as was the massive building with majestic columns and row upon row of windows. And, of course, the beautiful Nash statue of Queen Victoria. It was awe-inspiring to consider the longevity and history incorporated in this palace. She definitely needed to come back for a tour.

"Thanks," she said to Rick, blowing on her hands to warm them as the cold finally drove her to leave. "Ready for the fish and chips now?"

"You bet." Rick stopped a local to ask after a good pub, and minutes later they were seated at a scarred wooden table in a room crowded with tables and people. Soccer and rugby equipment along with player jerseys lined the walls while a rugby game played on several mounted TVs. In a back room a rowdy group erupted with cheers and groans.

"Dart tournament tonight, folks," a dark-haired waitress said as she stopped by the table. In her mid-forties, she was comfortably lush in a green T-shirt and blue jeans. "It'll be pretty loud."

"It's perfect." Savannah grinned at her. "I flat-out confess to being a tourist, so it's all part of the experience for me."

"Aye, and my guess is you'll be wanting some fish and chips and a pint. Where do you come to us from?"

"San Diego." Savannah rubbed her hands together. "Where it's much warmer this time of year. And yes, I'm going to be totally typical and get the fish and chips. And what the heck, I'll try the pint, too."

"You got it, doll. I'll bring you something pale." She turned her attention to Rick. Friendly when she spoke to Savannah, her gaze turned downright predatory as it ran over his body. "How about you, sweet thing?"

Savannah hid a smile behind her hand as red color flooded his cheeks.

He cleared his throat. "I'll have the same."

"Aye, and I'll bring you something dark." She shifted closer to him with a roll of well-rounded hips. "You look man enough to handle it."

With a lingering backward glance she disappeared into the crowd.

"Oh, she likes you," Savannah teased him. "Just let me know if you need me to make myself scarce."

"That woman just ate me alive with her eyes." He shook his finger at Savannah. "Under no circumstances are you to leave me alone with that cougar."

"Cougar?" She laughed. "Oh my, does she scare you?"

"I'm an intelligent man, so hell yeah."

She grinned. "Don't worry, I'll protect your virtue—or should I say manhood? I mean really, what if we were a couple?"

He pinned her with an intent stare. "Sweetheart, for the next hour, we are."

"What? You don't think she'd play by your *rules?*" How dangerous to play with him like this, but she couldn't resist.

"The rules are there so no one gets hurt." He defended his system with a flick of his eyes toward the bar and the woman under discussion. "She doesn't look like she's afraid of pain."

"It hurts so good?" she teased provocatively.

His gaze flashed back to her. "You're shocking me, Ms. Jones."

Yeah, she'd rather shocked herself. "You brought it up. Besides, I'm not as innocent as you seem to think."

"Sure you are," he assured her, certainty clear as crystal in his tone, "and it has nothing to do with how many lovers you've had. You're caring and giving. Genuine. You bring everyone around you to a higher level."

"Wow," she breathed, inordinately pleased by his assessment. She knew she got on his nerves sometimes and she was nowhere near his intellectual equal, so his comment touched her deeply. About to gush, she pulled herself back. He'd hate that. Instead she blessed him with a cheeky smile. "So you *do* like me."

He grinned and shook his head. "Sometimes."

"Uh-uh, be nice. Here comes the waitress with our food."

He lifted one dark brow. "Maybe you're not so innocent after all. You've got a mean streak."

"Oh, I bet I'm just a kitten next to the cougar."

"Just stay close."

"I will, I promise." She scooted back her chair. "As soon as I get back from the restroom."

"What?" he demanded in mock outrage. "Some friend you are."

"Come on, we both know you can handle her. Be right back."

She made quick work of her trip to the bathroom, not because she was worried about Rick—he could take care of himself. But she was having fun and didn't want to miss a minute of the adventure.

Over fish and chips they got involved in the rugby game, she rooting for Ireland while he cheered for Wales. The dart tournament got louder still, the waitress flirted some more and Savannah had a ball.

The game ended and they donned their coats

and walked down the street toward Buckingham Palace to catch a cab. It amazed her that some of the shops were still open, but when she glanced at her watch it was only seven.

"Wait. In here." Rick caught her hand. Startled by the searing touch she stopped in her tracks. He pulled her toward a leather and coat shop. "We can get you some gloves."

"Oh, no," She held back. "I'll find some closer to the hotel."

"Come on. Let's at least see what they have." He opened the door and ushered her inside.

The rich scent of leather pleasantly filled the small store. Savannah reluctantly followed Rick to the accessory section where he selected several pairs for her to try on. She did so, marveling at the suppleness and warmth. She particularly enjoyed a pair made of leather with a fleece lining; the quality and fit were exquisite. They were so soft, so warm she didn't want to take them off. But she must.

"Those are a nice fit," Rick said.

"Yes." A little sad, a little embarrassed, she pulled them off. "Rick, it's so nice of you to stop here, but, really, I can't afford these."

"But you like them?"

"Of course." She placed them back on the rack. "But that's not the point."

"It's exactly the point." He retrieved the gloves and handed them to the hovering clerk along with a pair of men's gloves. "We'll take both."

"Rick, no," Savannah protested. "I can't get these."

"You're not. I'm getting them."

Touched, she still shook her head. "I can't let you do that."

"You have no choice. They're a gift for your help today." He handed the clerk his credit card.

"Rick, this isn't necessary."

"I know. I want to get them for you." After pocketing his wallet he placed the bag in her hands. "Thank you."

"No, thank *you*." Letting the fun and ease of the evening direct her, she gave in to impulse and lifted onto her toes to kiss his cheek.

Desire flared in his eyes. He appeared to struggle with himself for a moment, then he lowered his head and covered her mouth with his. For one glorious minute he consumed her, drawing a response from her that met his passionate demand.

When he pulled back, she'd all but forgotten where she was.

While she regrouped, he ran a finger down her cheek. "My apologies. That's the last time that can happen."

Not quite able to wrap her tongue around words, she nodded mutely.

With a return to his stoic expression, he stepped back. "We should head back to the hotel."

Rick stared hard at his reflection in the mirror the next morning as he finished shaving. He didn't look any different. Didn't really feel different, but something was off.

Maybe it was jet lag or something in the water here in England, but there had to be an explanation for his uncharacteristic behavior. Playing tourist, flirting, kissing his assistant: Was he insane? He had no business having fun.

Okay, that was wrong. He deserved to have fun as much as the next guy. But not with Savannah. He had no business having fun with his assistant. The next time she wanted to play tourist she was on her own.

Huh, that thought certainly took the punch out of his day. He attributed the curious sense of letdown to delayed jet lag rather than to the disquieting notion of Savannah being out and about on her own. Not that she'd hesitate. The woman was fearless, which wasn't the same as being safe. Though the Lord knew she made friends wherever she went. Take the cougar last night. Propositioning him in the hallway one moment and laughing like old friends with Savannah the next.

He tossed down the towel and reached for his deodorant.

The problem was, he'd had a great time last night.

Watching the game, sharing the camaraderie of the crowd, eating the simple but good food. And with Savannah seated across from him making him laugh.

Swish and rinse. Finished, he dropped his toothbrush in a cup and set his shaving kit aside.

Again she'd made him laugh. He enjoyed the company of women, but they didn't engage him. He didn't let them. But Savannah slid under his guard and challenged him in so many ways.

But it had to stop. No more laughing, no more flirting, no more giving her gifts, and certainly no more nibbling on her plump bottom lip.

Now he felt downright deflated. Yes, it was definitely jet lag.

*　*　*

The phone was ringing when he entered the parlor suite. Savannah sat at the table eating muffins for breakfast. She began to rise, but he waved her off and answered the phone himself.

It was Crosse calling to set up an appointment for four that afternoon.

"His attorneys are going over the changes and they'll have a counteroffer to us within the next couple of days," Rick told Savannah after hanging up the phone. "We'll have two days to review and respond. He's hoping we'll be able to celebrate with dinner before we leave."

"That's great news," she enthused. "Did he say what the changes were?"

"No, but he said they were minor. I'm not expecting anything too shocking."

He was right. When the contract arrived and they reviewed the noted changes, most were in areas where Rick had already built in room for negotiation. Only one required him to get on the phone to the company attorney.

He and Savannah made a good team, taking care of the details and wrapping up loose ends. He felt great going into the meeting the next day.

His confidence was rewarded when an agreement was reached and the contracts were signed. The relief and satisfaction were huge, even more so than when he'd closed the deal with Emerson. Maybe because he'd come close to failing this time, something he wasn't used to, but he didn't think so; this fit felt right. He respected Crosse and they actually hit it off once they began to communicate properly.

He spent the rest of the week viewing properties and interviewing local contractors and vendors. He was so pleased with their progress he gave in to Savannah's wishes for some tourist time on their last day as long as she was back in time for dinner with the Crosses.

"I don't know where to start." All smiles, she headed straight for the stack of brochures she'd been collecting. Fanning them in front of her, she invited, "You choose."

He really wanted to—he'd had the best time at the pub with her their first night in London, and knew he'd have a blast jetting around town with her.

But… "You go on without me," he declined. "I have some loose ends to tie up here first." It was better this way. He'd already relaxed his standards around her more than with any other employee. He needed to rein himself in, which might be more boring but was safer all around.

He finished the bit of business he wanted to do and then wandered over to the Tower of London. A jeweler could hardly come to town without viewing the Crown Jewels. The Imperial State Crown was a marvel in itself. Over three thousand precious jewels—diamonds, emeralds, sapphires and rubies—manifested the majesty of the headpiece.

Yeah. "You are what you wear" was by no means a modern edict. A thought that proved true when he moved over to the display of royal armory. Fascinating stuff, but the third time he found himself turning to draw Savannah's attention to something and being frustrated when she wasn't there, he decided it was time to go.

Back at the hotel he freshened up and changed into a suit and tie and then opened his laptop to go through his emails while he waited for Savannah.

He'd been at it thirty minutes when the door to Savannah's room opened and she entered the room.

"I'm ready."

Rick glanced from the report he was reading to the clock in the corner of the screen. Excellent. They had fifteen minutes to get downstairs, where Crosse and his wife would pick them up.

Things were definitely looking up.

Until he glanced over and saw Savannah in a hot little black dress that made his mouth literally water. The dark color showcased her pale skin, while the swirl of the skirt and her spiked heels made her legs look as though they went on forever. And the shimmering peach lipstick painted on her lush lips tempted him to take a bite.

He was in *so* much trouble.

The Crosses had reservations for them at the Criterion restaurant, a jewel of Piccadilly Square since 1873. Stunned to be in one of London's finest restaurants, Savannah felt truly a part of this historic city. The glamour, sophistication and elegance made her feel special. The gilded ceilings, magnificent grand windows and towering arches were awe-inspiring. Gold and marble oozed lavishness from every angle, an excellent example of old-world grandeur and timeless elegance.

Crossing her ankles under the table, Savannah silently thanked Claudia for insisting she bring the little black dress on her trip. The silky slide of the material over her body gave her confidence, something she desperately needed with Albert's wife, Paulette, sitting across from her.

Beautiful, elegant and well-spoken, the woman epitomized everything Savannah wanted to be and fell short of.

Feeling out of her depth she was prepared to slide into the background but Paulette, both gracious and friendly, drew her into the conversation. Savannah held her own, and she soon relaxed, enjoying a glass of wine while laughing and chatting as the meal progressed.

The men had ordered brandy when the conversation turned to the properties they'd toured. Savannah switched to coffee and listened. As they talked, it became clear Rick had narrowed his choice down to two.

She watched as he lifted a snifter to his mouth. The muscles in his throat worked as he swallowed. Her mouth watered.

"Rett would like the property at our hotel best," Savannah blurted out, to distract her thoughts from the deliciousness that was her boss.

Mention of his twin brought a frown to Rick's brow. She'd never known two men closer than the brothers, but they had very different business styles.

"My twin brother," he clarified for the Crosses. "He's in charge of purchasing and design."

Paulette touched the diamond choker at her neck. "I'm familiar with his work."

"Is that one of Rett's pieces?" Savannah asked. "I've been admiring it all night."

"I love it." Paulette affectionately patted Crosse's hand on the table. "Albert picked it up for me when he was in San Diego for the discussions last spring. Why do you say Rett would prefer the Knightsbridge property?"

"It's smaller than the other property, but it has more character and more windows, which allows for more natural lighting, plus more display space."

"Security is more important than setting." Rick stated the age-old argument between the brothers.

"Not to Rett," she said simply.

He half turned toward her, hooking an elbow on the back of his chair "You're *my* assistant— your loyalty should be to me."

"But he's teaching me design." She shifted so she faced him. "And he's not here to represent his view."

"If he asks again, tell him I've got it covered," Rick suggested. "He'll listen to you, since obviously he likes you."

"Oh, no, you're not using me to misdirect him."

"How delightful." Paulette clapped her hands, drawing Savannah and Rick's attention.

Both the Crosses smiled at them. Paulette shared a laughing glance with Albert. "Don't they make a lovely couple? Remember when we used to bicker like that? Oh, you loved to give me a bad time."

Crosse winked at his wife. "Spot-on. You rose so beautifully to the bait." Nodding to Savannah and Rick, Albert said, "She still does."

"Oh, no." Savannah jumped in to correct the wrong impression. "I'm just Rick's assistant."

"And I was in the secretarial queue when Albert found me," Paulette said.

Startled by that revelation, Savannah blurted, "But you went to college, right?"

Paulette shook her blond head. "I started in reception right out of school. My family had no funds for university. But that didn't matter to Albert."

"I never went to university. Why should it matter to me if she did? After our boys were out of nappies, she got her degree in art history. Now she's assistant curator at the Museum of Modern Art."

"Albert, stop." Paulette flushed with pleasure. "They're not interested in hearing about me."

Actually, Savannah found it very intriguing. She'd been thinking of going back to school, and here was a beautiful, intelligent woman who had got her degree after she began her family. It motivated Savannah to act on her dream.

Working at Sullivans' with Rick gave her a sense of confidence she'd lacked for a long time. It had brought her to this fabulous restaurant with these gracious, sophisticated people. How much further could it take her?

"It's an amazing accomplishment." She smiled at Paulette. "Was it hard?"

The older woman winced, but there was pride in her expression, as well. "It was worth it," she said. "But we were talking about you two."

"No, really—"

"It's obvious you have feelings for each other." Albert patted his wife's hand fondly. "We've been together for thirty-two years. Good years. The heart of your family comes from your commitment to each other. But I'm here to tell you the key to any successful relationship is compromise."

"It's true," Paulette confirmed softly. "The love you share creates the core of your family. The heart comes from working together, supporting each other."

They were so sweet, so earnest, Savannah bit her lip to keep from blurting out the truth. Or laughing out loud at their mistake. She wasn't sure which would come out if she let go. She didn't dare meet Rick's gaze.

"Don't be fooled—it takes work. Sometimes

it's really difficult, but the kids, and always having someone there for you, make the journey worth it." Dignified and proud, Albert stood and helped his wife to her feet. "And I know what hard workers you are, so you're halfway there."

Savannah shook her head.

"There's no use denying it, dear." Paulette graced both Savannah and Rick with a smile as she joined her husband. "I can see you're meant for each other."

Albert glanced between the two of them and nodded. "She's rarely wrong about these things." He reached for his wife's hand. "Rick, I know you have something planned, so we'll leave you here." The men shook hands. "I look forward to working with you both."

"It was lovely meeting you." Savannah stood to give Paulette a friendly hug. "Thank you for coming out to celebrate with us."

"My pleasure. You're such a charming couple. I'm sure we will all work well together."

"Paulette—"

"We're grateful for your well wishes. Aren't we, darling?" Rick picked her hand up from the table and carried it to his mouth. The heat of his breath on her skin, then the touch of his lips caused her mouth to go dry.

Vaguely, she heard Paulette giggle in delight as she walked away.

Savannah cleared her throat, made a tentative effort to pull her hand free. "Why?"

He retained his grip on her; in fact, he turned her hand over and pressed his lips to the sensitive skin of her wrist.

Oh my.

Unprepared for his sensual assault, she yanked her hand away and buried it along with her other hand in her lap. "What are you doing?"

Happy with life, no doubt helped along by the

wine and brandy, he grinned. "Come on, we made her day."

Enough already. She found the constant buzz of sexual tension between her and Rick exhausting. And he thought it would be amusing to play sensual games?

He wanted to play? Well, she'd show him she knew how to throw a hardball.

"I understand." She drained the last sip of wine. "You were just flirting for your audience."

He inclined his head, the overhead light gleaming in the dark sheen of his hair. Humor lit his blue eyes, inviting her to enjoy the moment. "They wanted lovers, I gave them lovers. It ends things on a positive note."

"I see." Beyond being amused, she stood and slowly leaned toward him. The closer she got, the more wary his gaze became.

Wise man.

The kiss they'd shared on the plane never

strayed far from her mind, and her inner diva demanded she remind him exactly why it was dangerous to play with fire. Standing over him, she cupped his face in her hands and pressed her lips to his.

Slowly, softly, she kissed him.

Oh my, indeed.

When she raised her head, desire burned in his eyes. He reached for her. She stepped back, then licked her lips.

Yeah, she'd shown him.

She turned to find the whole room watching. She literally felt the pink rush to her face. Passion made her movements sluggish as she picked up her purse and jacket. "Good night. *Darling.*"

CHAPTER SEVEN

OF COURSE, he ruined her great exit by following her. Savannah dodged him by stepping into the restroom. *Good night. Darling.* Right. What had she been thinking?

Obviously, she hadn't thought. She'd reacted.

He'd looked so pleased with himself. Sitting there so calm and composed with no hint that his outrageous gesture had shaken him at all when it had rocked her to the very core. Now she just felt foolish.

But she couldn't hide forever.

She left the restroom. Rick stood in the lobby, holding her coat and scarf.

"That was a miserable end to an otherwise delightful dinner." Even to her it sounded like an accusation. She cocked her head and decided that suited her just fine.

"Don't you think you're overreacting?" he countered.

"No. What did Crosse mean you have something planned? Should I make my own way back to the hotel?" she asked, changing the subject.

"I have a surprise for our last night here." He helped her into her coat.

She scowled, in no mood to go anywhere with him. "I don't like surprises."

"Really? I thought you'd love surprises." Undeterred, he swept her along, ushering her outside into the crisp night air.

"I used to."

"You'll like this one," he insisted as he hailed a taxi.

A short while later she slowly climbed out of the car, her gaze locked on the huge Millennium Wheel. "Okay, I'm surprised."

"They say at night it's like you're right in the middle of the stars," he said, excitement obvious in his voice.

It caused her to stop and really look at him. He'd removed his jacket and stood there looking a little rumpled, his hair slightly disheveled, his eyes shining with anticipation.

"I've rented a private flight for us." Rubbing his hands together, he led the way into the terminal.

With a sigh, she put aside her embarrassment and annoyance, unable to deflate his rare show of enthusiasm.

Still, nerves got the better of her as the time came to board. "Oh, Rick. I don't know. I'm not sure I'm this brave."

He simply held out his hand for hers. "If there's one thing I've learned about you, Savannah, it's that you're fearless."

She looked at his outstretched hand. Did he really believe that? How she wished it were true. She wasn't fear*less*; she just didn't let her fears stop her. Except when it came to school— maybe because she wanted it so badly? Another hint it was time to stop procrastinating.

She bit her lip. Not so fearless when it came to flying either.

"Do you trust me?" he asked softly.

"Oh." She released her pent-up breath in a resigned sigh. "Yes, of course."

"Then let me give you the stars."

Oh, man. How did she resist that?

"Okay, but if you have to carry me around tomorrow because of my shattered knees, just remember you insisted."

"I'll keep you safe."

The promise issued in his forthright manner was enough to cause her knees to melt, so maybe she wouldn't have any problems after all.

The trip more than lived up to his claims. An attendant accompanied them yet stayed discreetly in the background. Champagne and strawberries immediately helped to lighten her tension.

Rick stood directly behind her, close enough to touch yet always at a distance. Quietly keeping his word.

"It's so quiet," she observed.

"That's probably because there are no other people around," he said dryly.

She flicked him a reproachful gaze. "It's not that. There's a stillness up here."

He moved to her side. "Yeah. I feel it, too."

"The view is magnificent." Watching the lights of the city expand outward made the gradual rise into the dark an exciting adventure. "It's like we're flying among the stars."

"When I promise a woman the stars, I deliver."

"Yes, you do." She laughed up into his blue eyes. "Thank you for insisting."

Desire flared between them, practically sizzling in the air.

A finger under her chin lifted her head up to his, and he fitted his mouth to hers. Closing her eyes she saw more stars as he made her world twirl in wild abandon.

This night was a dream come true even while she knew it was too good to be true. She knew she should question his uncharacteristic change of attitude. But it felt too wonderful standing in the middle of the heavens with her head on his chest.

So she wouldn't ask, wouldn't question. She'd simply hold on tight and live in the moment. And when they left England tomorrow, she'd have an unbelievable memory of more than this fabulous city that had captured her heart.

He spun her around so her back snugged against his front and they both faced the view.

"So, what put you off surprises?" he asked huskily.

Oh. The question brought up painful memories of promises made and broken, of surprises dangled but never coming to fruition. She loved her father, but she'd been disappointed so many times she'd lost her faith in him, and she didn't know if she'd ever get it back, which saddened her. She refused to be sad tonight; she'd just vowed to live in the moment. And this was where it had taken her.

"Experience," she answered softly. "When they don't come off, it's more painful and disappointing than if you'd never gotten your hopes up in the first place."

"Ouch. Your dad?"

She nodded. "When my mom got sick my dad disappeared from our lives. Not literally—he came home each night, but emotionally he was disconnected." She lifted her eyes to meet his. "Actually I give him credit—he was there for Mom right through to the end. But it took all he had. He shut the rest of us out."

"Rough times. I know from Gram your mom has been gone for a while. You must have been very young."

"Fourteen when she got sick, seventeen when she passed. Dad didn't even make my high-school graduation. He just buried himself in work."

His arms tightened around her. "The workaholic you once mentioned."

"Yes. Claudia and Daniel were younger, four and five years younger than me, but it didn't take them long to figure out Dad was unavailable."

"It was different for them. They had you. I know what a difference that makes because we had Gram."

"Thank you, that helps a lot."

Tonight was turning into so much more than she'd ever anticipated. She felt closer to Rick than ever before. They talked about everything and nothing. He made her laugh, he made her want, and when he talked of his father, he nearly made her cry.

"We went fishing and he played ball with us. He came to our games when he could. I thought he was the best dad in the world."

"Sure sounds like it." It made her remember the early days, when her own father made time to be with the family.

"Yeah, I only learned the truth about the business failing when I watched Gram pick up the pieces after he and my mom died. If she weren't such a cagey old gal, we would have lost everything."

"So you're complaining because he spent time with you?"

"He should have taken care of business instead. Sure, it was fun to play catch. It wouldn't have been fun to lose our house." He released her to grab them two glasses of champagne. "We were two payments behind on the mortgage payments when he died. We went to live with Gram and she sold the house, put the money into the business. It saved us."

And changed him forever. At the age of nine or ten he'd lost the man he'd worshipped and learned that he'd been a dreamer rather than a businessman. The worst of all possible sins to Rick. No wonder he worked so hard. It was in compensation for the damage done by his father, and a tribute to the sacrifices made by his grandmother.

"He loved you. Chose you and your brothers over his job." She laid a hand over his. "That says a lot."

"It says he was weak."

"No," she said softly, "it says you were more important to him than a store."

"It was our livelihood. And the store had been in my family for over seventy years. Built on the sweat of my father's father, grandfather and great-grandfather." He turned his hand over to lace his fingers with hers. "You're too easy to talk to, and I've revealed too much. No one knows about the late mortgage but Gram and I."

"Your secret is safe with me." She focused on her wineglass, circling the rim with a fingertip. "Divided loyalties—that's a hard lesson to learn so young. Have you never wanted more from life then? Never believed you could fall in love *and* run a successful business?"

Rick took the question on the chin. He should have known when he took the conversation to a personal level that Savannah would draw more from him than he found comfortable. For some reason he felt compelled to know more about her, to ferret out her secrets. It was only fair to give up some of his own in return.

He knew love; his family abounded in it. Yet he'd always felt apart from the closeness that held them all together. Perhaps his resentment for their father had something to do with it. Or maybe he just feared losing anyone else.

"No. I haven't always been so resistant to relationships. In college a pretty little blonde from Boston caught my attention enough that I asked her to marry me. She accepted, but in the end she missed her family and chose to return east."

Savannah turned in his arms to look up at him. He saw a hundred more questions in her eyes and braced himself.

"Did you consider going after her?"

"I thought about it. But it came down to this—she didn't love me enough to stay. I didn't love her enough to follow. The breakup still hurt, though."

"I'm sure it did. If there's one thing I've learned about you, Rick, it's that you feel things deeper than you let on."

How could she possibly know that? It was something he'd buried long ago. Feelings were messy and distracting. He preferred things simple and straightforward and that's how he'd built his life.

"I'm sorry you gave up on love. I think you have a lot to offer."

"Sir." The attendant stood a few feet away. "The flight will be docking in a few minutes. We'll need you to be ready to exit."

Rick nodded and the man returned to his station. They'd been so intent on each other, they hadn't noticed the flight was over. And so was their time alone.

Tomorrow it would be back to business.

Back in the hotel suite, Savannah pulled off her gloves and scarf. She glanced at Rick through her lashes. He was much closer than she'd expected and she had to run her gaze over his broad chest to reach his eyes.

"Thank you for the lovely surprise. I'll never forget tonight."

"I'm not ready for it to end." He caught her hand and pulled her to him. Slowly, he lowered his head, his lips settling softly against hers.

Oh my. She held still, afraid to move, not because she feared him, but because she didn't want him to stop. Giving in to the temptation of his mouth on hers, she touched the tip of her tongue to his bottom lip. Immediately he angled his head and took the kiss to a new level. He tasted of man and champagne, an intoxicating mix.

And a potent reminder of the alcohol he'd consumed through dinner and the flight. That they'd both consumed.

Regretfully, she turned her head, breaking off contact. "We should stop."

"Do you want to stop?" His breath heated the skin of her temple.

No, not at all, her heart cried, though her head said different. "You won't be happy about this in the morning."

"Define *happy.* Life is mostly the same old, same old with rare moments of extreme pleasure." He traced the shell of her ear with his tongue. "I think we can reach new levels of extreme."

As skillful fingers played down her sides, she fully believed him. He whispered in her ear that he had protection.

"This is so wrong." But she lifted her mouth to his, meeting him halfway, threading her fingers through the short strands of his dark hair.

"Yeah, but it feels so right." He sealed his mouth over hers, ending the conversation.

Opening her mouth under his, she let him in, let him sweep away her protests. She held him to her, breathing in his scent, man and soap with a hint of spice. He smelled as good as he tasted.

He demanded and she gave willingly, lifting onto her toes to get closer. He nibbled her lower lip then soothed the bite with a swipe of his tongue. She moaned as he worked his way down her jaw and then her neck, to her shoulder and lower. She shivered at each bite, sighed with each soothing caress.

Passion eclipsed common sense as she practically climbed him to deepen the embrace, and he helped by circling her waist with one strong arm and lifting her against him, her feet several inches off the ground. She wrapped her arms around his neck and let him carry her to his room. One high heel fell off and she kicked away the other.

"Business is over for the day."

Once she gained her feet again, she took delight in removing his tie, pulling hand over hand until it hung loose in her fingers. Feeling wicked she tossed it over her shoulder and reached for the buttons of his shirt.

For each one she released, she kissed the warm skin revealed until he lost patience and stripped off the shirt himself. Next he made short work of sliding down her zipper and the little black dress pooled on the floor.

They sank to the bed where the tension smoldering below the surface exploded in sizzling passion.

Some called him cold, unfeeling, but she'd always seen his intensity, his deep sense of duty. It drove his ambition and dedication, which, in turn, fueled his isolation. But cold and unfeeling? Not by a long shot. By turns tender and demanding, he fanned the flames of her desire hotter and hotter.

He was in the shower when she woke up. With mixed feelings, she escaped to her room to shower, dress and complete her packing. And then they were in a taxi on the way to the airport.

In a blink they were back on a plane on the last leg of the flight home. Another red-eye flight. She hoped they didn't encounter turbulence as bad as on her first flight.

Tired but anxious, she shifted in her seat.

"You've been quiet," Rick said. "Do you think you'll be able to sleep?"

She blinked at him. "Wow. Déjà vu. I hope that doesn't mean we'll have bad turbulence."

He looked away, and she rolled her eyes in rueful amusement, not surprised by his avoidance of emotional discourse.

"Don't worry. I'm not going to get clingy," she reassured him. "In fact, I want to thank you for an awesome trip. I had a great time."

"Yes. It was a very successful trip. Even Rett should be happy."

"I'm glad it worked out for the company, but I was talking about us. I do understand that it all ends when we touch down in San Diego."

He turned back to her, relief clear in his eyes. "Oh, I think I can see you to your door."

"Such a gentleman." She smiled, careful to keep the growing sorrow from showing. He would have done that anyway. "Your grandmother would be proud of you."

He flinched slightly, just a quick narrowing of the eyes and she wondered at the moment of vulnerability. Maybe he wasn't as unmoved by the end of their fling as he wanted her to think.

"I'm going to miss you," she said softly.

His gaze flicked to hers. "We'll be working together every day."

"Of course." And the proximity would make things harder not easier.

"Are you going to be all right with that?" he pressed.

"Yes." She nodded, emphatically. "Last night was indescribable, but I'm not really the kind of girl to enjoy flings. And when I find the right man I want to know I'm number one for him. That when it comes to priorities and split loyalties, I come first. I told you about how my father turned to work for solace so maybe you can understand that. I know he loves me. It just doesn't always feel like it."

"And you think that's how I treat the women in my life?" he asked thoughtfully.

"Yes," she answered honestly and saw that flash of vulnerability in him again. "But it's okay, because that's the life you've chosen. You've said you don't plan to get married. I respect that. But I also hope you find someone who'll fulfill you more than well-balanced profit statements."

"Thanks. I think."

She forced another smile and lowered her gaze to their hands, separated by several inches on the console between their first-class seats, and thought, *That's the way it has to be.* But she closed her eyes, shutting out the sight.

"I think I will try to sleep."

He said nothing, but a moment later his hand covered hers.

CHAPTER EIGHT

"SAVANNAH, I'll be at the downtown branch for a few hours, and then I'm off the clock until four." Rick stopped at her desk to give her his schedule. "Call me if you need me."

"I thought you were attending the meeting with human resources for the proposal from the independent health-care provider this afternoon."

"I changed my mind."

"Really?" she blurted in surprise and then quickly tried to recoup. "I mean did you want me to sit in on the meeting and take notes?"

"No. The manager can handle it." Instead of leaving he stood jiggling the change in his pocket. "Aren't you having lunch with Jesse today?"

"Yes. How did you know about that?"

He lifted a dark brow, silently reminding her Jesse was family. "Are you going to talk to her about her teacher's certification?"

"Maybe."

"You are."

She looked at him from under her lashes. "Don't push me."

"You should talk to human resources. We pay for continuing education for our employees."

Okay, she just shook her head at that. "I'm a temp, remember? And teaching is not continuing ed for jewelry-making, consumer marketing or retail sales."

He inclined his head. "There's design. You have a real talent in that direction."

"I thought of that, but I want to teach. Plus, I'm still only a temp."

The man was driving her insane. The stoic, distancing man from before their trip to England had returned with a vengeance upon touchdown in San Diego a month ago. Which she'd expected, of course. And she'd prepared herself for his reappearance. Not that it had been easy to switch gears from lover to assistant when she was suffering from jet lag.

But on odd occasions this solicitous man popped up, and she truly didn't know what to make of him.

"Unless you're offering me a permanent position here at Sullivans'?" she prompted.

"A permanent position?" he drawled in speculation.

The expressions fleeting across his face reflected the way she felt, a combination of horror followed by hope replaced by resignation. Which told her his customary cold shoulder was as much a facade as her daily display of disinterest.

The chemistry between them blazed as strongly now as it had in England. And before that if she was honest.

Honest? Who was she kidding? If he were to offer her a permanent job, she'd probably jump on it even though she told herself nightly she'd be out of here and away from the temptation of Rick Sullivan in a heartbeat if it weren't for her obligation to Mrs. Sullivan to see the job assignment through to the end.

Yep, that's what she told herself. And at night she meant it, but during the day she longed for the sight of him, shivered at the sound of his deep voice. More than once she'd caught herself leaning closer to get a whiff of his cologne and the underlying scent of man.

When he was around, that is. Since their return to the States, he'd hit the road to visit all the branch offices. This was his second trip downtown.

"I don't get you, Rick." Frustration made her speak up. "I can't tell if you want me to stay or you're trying to get rid of me."

He pinned her with an intense, unreadable

gaze. "Good question. When I figure it out, you'll be the first to know." And flipping the marble hourglass, he turned and walked out of the office.

She glared after his retreating back. No mixed signals there.

And lunch with Jesse only added to her confusion. For all his recent travels, it seemed Rick had made time to spend time with his family.

"I don't know what happened in England." Jesse flashed Savannah a knowing glance. "But Rick is like a new man."

"Really?" Savannah twisted her iced-tea glass on the table, avoiding eye contact. "In what way?"

"He's more visible, more available. This afternoon he's playing handball with Brock. And it's been great to have him at Sunday dinners again. I can tell you Gram's thrilled."

"Family means a lot to him." Savannah thought of his willingness to sacrifice a family of his own to protect the interests of the whole. "That's not new."

"No, but he's always been a little aloof. I mean, he makes the big events, but usually only gets to Sunday dinner three or four times a year." Jesse sat back, allowing the waiter room to deliver her meal. "Something definitely happened to shake him up in England."

"He's very excited about the international deal." Feeling a tad nauseous, Savannah pushed the club salad around on her plate. "It was an important goal for him."

"Hmm." Jesse nodded over a bite of Chinese chicken salad. "He's invited everyone to the London opening in November. I can hardly wait. But enough about Rick, except to say keep on doing whatever you're doing. Let's talk about you. I love to teach, so I'm happy to share anything you want to know. Do you have a field of study you want to specialize in?"

The talk turned to education, both learning

and teaching, but in the back of Savannah's mind lurked the thought that his trip to Europe may well have changed Rick. She knew he'd been impressed with Crosse and his style of doing business.

She'd certainly come back a different person, both in heart and spirit. Paulette's story had inspired Savannah to act on her desire to go back to school. And in giving herself to Rick she'd opened herself to him more than to any other man she'd known.

Too bad she was a woman who needed to know she came first in her man's life, and he was a man driven by ghosts to see his company succeed.

When it came down to essentials those were two things that weren't going to change.

She'd be a fool to believe anything else. No matter how much she wished things were different.

Feeling totally sick, she pushed her plate away.

* * *

Dazed and confused took on new meaning as Savannah stared at the plus sign on the little white stick. Equally excited and horrified she finally acknowledged her suspicions were correct. Still carrying the stick she moved into her bedroom.

"I'm pregnant." She tested the words and found they made her knees weak.

"Oh, Savannah." Claudia was right there lending Savannah strength, walking her to the bed to sit. "It's going to be okay."

She sank to the edge of the mattress when she'd rather crawl into the middle and hide her head under the covers.

"I'm expecting the boss's baby. That's really *not* okay," she said in a strangled voice.

"Don't panic. That was only one test. Maybe it's wrong. We'll get another one, or two. We'll get three more tests and try again. I'm sure it's just a mistake."

"It's not a mistake. I've been sick in the afternoons, and I'm constantly tired. I have to stop pretending it's not real."

"The flu is going around. I've heard a lot of people misread these tests—"

"Claudia, this is the third test I've taken."

She'd been in denial for nearly a month before buying the first test. She'd honestly thought she had the flu. As Claudia said, there were some nasty ones going around. Plus Savannah had kept reminding herself they'd used protection, and she was on the pill, so she couldn't be pregnant.

"Oh." Claudia took in Savannah's announcement. Then the questions began. "But how? You're on the pill right?"

"Yes, but I've thought about that. I'm usually very good about taking the pills at the same time every day, because the doctor said that was most effective, but with the long flights and time change I figure I missed a whole day and then I was on London time. I'm sure it got messed up."

"But you said you used protection."

Savannah bit her lip and looked at Claudia through her lashes. "We talked about using protection. It definitely got mentioned at one point. But I just don't know." She rubbed at her temples as if trying to massage the memories back. "After we moved to the bedroom I don't remember anything but the really hot sex."

"Now you're just bragging." Claudia grinned.

"Really. Hot. Sex. Three times."

"Savannah!" Claudia exclaimed, happily scandalized. "You're a red-hot mama. I'm so proud of you."

"Not exactly the reaction I'm looking for."

"Sweetie, you're a bit of a prude, probably because you had to take on the mother's role with Daniel and me. And we both know you stink at flirting. I'm just happy you found someone that saw beyond all that. You deserve to have fun."

"I guess I can't even do fun right, because it sure seems like it comes at a high price." Savannah swiped a tear from the corner of her eye.

"Well, I see this as a blessing." Claudia rubbed a soothing hand up and down Savannah's back. "No one will make a better mother than you."

"You're so sweet." She mustered a smile for her sister. "But I need to get through the panic stage before I can start seeing blessings. I just enrolled at National University. I finally make the decision to go back to school and suddenly I'm back to raising a family again. Oh, God." Savannah wrung her hands. "How am I going to tell Rick? He is going to freak out."

"Come on, he's a stand-up guy. I'm sure he'll handle this with integrity."

"Phff," Savannah huffed. "You got that right. He's strong on duty and responsibility. I see a marriage proposal coming, and I so don't want that."

"Wait. I thought you were worried you'd have to do the whole single-parent thing on your own? You just said you want to continue your schooling. The man has money, looks, and ethics and you don't want to marry him?" Claudia waved the little stick. "You obviously have chemistry and motivation, so what's the problem?"

"The problem is I deserve to be *loved,* to have an equal partner in the marriage. I don't want to settle for less."

"No, and you shouldn't. But do you want to raise this baby alone?" Hearing how that sounded, Claudia quickly added. "I mean, of course, I'll be there to help."

"Stop, I know what you mean. The problem is Rick's sense of duty might prompt him to propose, but I don't see him being a lot of help. He has issues and work is his coping mechanism. Jesse says he's changed, but I haven't seen it. He makes our dad look like a happy homemaker."

"Don't you think you're being a little harsh?"

"No."

"You're scared."

Now there was an understatement. "I really am."

Claudia leaned her head on Savannah's shoulder. "What are you going to do?"

Good question. Much as she might want to there'd be no burying her head in the covers, no hiding from this. She may not have chosen to have a child, but a life beat within her. It was time to man up.

Savannah patted her belly. "I'm going to have a baby. But first I'm going to quit my job."

Savannah felt sick to her stomach. She'd been nauseous all morning. Neither crackers nor soda had helped. Nor had the meager bites of sandwich she'd managed to eat at lunch.

Today she intended to give Rick her notice of resignation. In fact, she'd already printed it out; she just needed to find it. She'd been scatterbrained all morning, stressing over the upcoming confrontation.

In the past month she'd chosen a doctor and had the pregnancy confirmed. And she'd looked for and accepted a new job as a department assistant for a private school.

She'd miss Sullivans' Jewels, but she felt it best to get out from under Rick's authority before she told him about the baby. He could be ruthless, and she wanted to be in a position of strength, to show him she was capable of providing for her child. Maybe not to the level his money would allow, but then she didn't intend cutting him out of the child's life. He could be as involved as he wanted to be.

From a distance.

Not that they'd be having that discussion today. She'd decided to wait to tell him about the baby until she was further along. Yes, it was a selfish decision, but she was the one carrying this baby. In this instance she needed to put herself first.

A baby's cry gave her an odd sense of déjà vu. The sound came again as she reached Rick's open door.

He stood at his desk in his shirtsleeves, hands on hips, staring with bemused frustration at the baby kicking in the carrier on his desk.

He looked up as she appeared in the doorway. "Good, you're back."

"Is Jesse with Rett again?" she asked.

"Yes. And thanks to you, she seems to think I welcome these opportunities to spend time with Troy."

"And so you should." She ventured a step into the room. Considering her current situation, she found the circumstances fascinating. "He's your nephew and the new addition to the family. How long has he been here?"

"Twenty minutes. He just woke up. And as for being new to the family, now most of my brothers are married new additions pop out on a regular basis."

She frowned at his cavalier comment. "That doesn't mean each child isn't special in his or her own right."

"No, but they're all pretty much the same at this age. I usually don't engage with them until they're able to talk."

"You're wrong. They're individuals from the moment they're born." She rounded the desk to smile down at Troy, who continued to kick at his carrier. "It's amazing to watch their personalities develop right before your eyes."

"Huh." He cocked his head as if acknowledging the info and then stepped back and gestured her forward. "All Troy appears to be developing is a fit."

"Oh, no." Savannah caught Rick's arm and drew him back in front of the baby, the first voluntary contact she'd had with him since returning to the States two and a half months ago.

The flex of muscle under her fingers revealed his awareness of the moment. She ignored her reaction and his.

"This is the perfect time to get better acquainted. He just wants up."

"Up?" Rick scowled, the gaze he flicked her way revealing an uncharacteristic uncertainty.

"He wants out of the carrier."

He glanced back at the baby. "He's locked in."

"It's not locked." Amused, she rolled her eyes at him. "It's just a few buckles. I'm sure you can figure it out."

Challenged, he made quick work of releasing the buckles. Troy squealed and kicked harder, excited by the signs of freedom. But Rick froze once he had the belts loosened.

"He won't break," Savannah reassured him. "Just hold him with confidence."

"I really don't have time for this. I have a meeting with Anderson."

"It's not for another hour."

Still he hesitated.

"Coward."

His blue eyes flashed a warning. She didn't care. What could he do, fire her? Not a big threat with her letter of resignation waiting to be found somewhere on her desk.

Her stomach churned at the thought of the coming discussion.

The goading worked. Rick bent and carefully lifted Troy out of his seat. Clearly uncomfortable, Rick held the boy with both hands away from his body.

Thrilled by his new position, Troy kicked his feet and reached for Rick, connecting with his nose.

"See. He likes you."

"Yeah." Removing the little hand from his nose, Rick placed a strong hand under the baby's butt and bounced the little one up and down.

Troy squealed and giggled and Rick shot her

a look of triumph, his smile almost as big as Troy's.

"Very nice. I'll just leave you two to get to know each other." Seeing him with the baby, watching him find joy in the child's delight, threw her into an emotional retreat.

"No," he ordered, his tone just short of panicked.

Troy frowned at the sharp bark of Rick's command.

"Don't go." Rick smiled and bounced the baby, quickly gaining control of himself. The sheepish look he sent Savannah held a plea. "We're not ready to fly solo yet."

Even more than before she longed to flee to the safety of her desk, his vulnerability touching her in ways that weakened her resolve, making him more approachable than he'd been in months.

She didn't want to see the warm, funny man she'd gotten to know in Europe. Far easier to walk away from the stern taskmaster she knew outside of their trip.

Though it cost her, she stayed while he and Troy got accustomed to each other. He knew the basics, having watched others handle the babies in the family, and he had good instincts. He didn't really need her, which unaccountably hurt.

And when Jesse called to say she'd be up in a minute to fetch Troy, Savannah made good her escape.

Angry at the irrational emotions warring within her, she began an extensive search for the missing letter of resignation. The sooner she got away from Rick, the better.

Jesse came and went with a cheerful wave. Savannah absently smiled and wished her well while pawing through the files piled on her desk. The letter had to be here somewhere.

A few minutes later a familiar paper landed

in front of her. "You want to explain this?" a deep male voice demanded.

Savannah jumped, her elbow connected with a folder and papers flew every which way.

With an arched brow, Rick bent to gather the loose papers, which he carefully handed her. She reached for them, but he held firm until she raised her eyes to meet his. Determination deepened the blue in his. "Is there something you want to tell me?"

"Obviously you read the letter. It's pretty clear." Her stomach roiled as she realized this was it, no more delaying the inevitable.

"Don't play dumb, Savannah. It doesn't become you."

True. It didn't sit well either. So she'd go on the offense. "You had to see this coming."

"You're leaving for 'personal reasons.'" A storm brewed in his eyes. "How convenient."

"No, actually, it's quite inconvenient," she denied with more vehemence than she knew she harbored. "It wasn't an easy decision to leave. I've enjoyed working for Sullivans'. And working on the international deal. I've learned a lot from you. So no, none of this has been convenient for me at all."

"Your personal reasons being you're uncomfortable spending time with me?" he asked in a deceptively conversational tone.

She wasn't fooled. The more reasonable he appeared, the more upset he was. And how like him to go right to the heart of the problem.

"Yes."

"I thought we were handling the situation just fine."

"You barely speak to me." She rubbed at an ache forming behind her right eye. "We communicate by email, voice mail and the occasional sticky note," she said dryly.

"It's working."

"It is so *not* working. What's happening is

you're doing more than usual, which leaves me twiddling my thumbs and you cranky."

"I haven't been cranky."

She lifted her brows at him and folded her hands on her desk. "Believe me, you've been cranky."

She'd dreaded the conversation because it skirted the issue of their night of passion, a topic she wanted to avoid if possible to keep him from suspecting the news she wanted to keep hidden.

What she hadn't expected was for him to argue with her.

She sat back in her chair and folded her arms over her chest. "Why are you fighting me on this?"

"I don't want to have to train another assistant. Especially when there's no valid reason for you to leave."

Frustrated and feeling sick, she said through clenched teeth, "You aren't listening to me."

"You haven't said anything worth listening to."

"Right." She finally gave in, realizing there'd be no relenting until he got his answers. She stood and walked past him into his office where she turned and confronted him after he closed the door. "Here's the truth. You may have been able to erase the time we spent together from your memory, but I haven't been so successful. So I felt it best to move on."

"Just like that?" he demanded. "Two weeks' notice and you're gone?"

"It's for the best. Training a new assistant will be better than continuing to fight the attraction we have no intention of acting on." She sighed, torn. But she wouldn't lie to him. "You know I'm right."

He frowned, his internal struggle obvious. "Do you want an apology?"

Confused, she cocked her head. "For what?"

"London—"

"No," she abruptly cut him off, and then swallowed against a wave of sickness. "I don't want an apology."

"Then what do you want?"

"Nothing. Oh, no." Suddenly the nerves and nausea got to her and she felt her stomach protesting. She breathed deeply, hoping it would settle. No such luck.

"No, no, no." She clapped a hand over her mouth and flew to his executive bathroom where she tossed up the meager contents of her stomach.

Embarrassed on top of being sick, she reached new levels of mortification when Rick's black loafers appeared at the edge of the toilet.

"Go away," she implored him.

"Shh." He smoothed a hand down her back and then held the hair away from her face when she bent forward again.

Sweat broke out on her forehead at the same time chills racked her body. Retching turned to dry heaves and she welcomed the strength of his hold as she shuddered under the assault on her system.

Finally she straightened, and he handed her a glass of water, which she accepted gratefully.

"I'm okay. Thank you." She braced her hands on the counter, carefully avoiding her reflection in the mirror. "Can I have a few minutes alone?"

"Sure." With a soft stroke of his fingers, he tucked her hair behind her ear. "Take your time."

"Oh, Mama." Savannah moaned once the door closed behind him. That last gentle touch had almost undone all her resolve. And it had reminded her of just how tender and caring he'd been in England.

She very much feared she'd given away a part of her heart she might never get back.

In the cupboard she found toothpaste and a new toothbrush and used both. She didn't even try to save her makeup. A damp cloth felt good on her clammy skin, but the lack of cosmetics left her feeling doubly exposed when she returned to Rick's office.

He wasn't at his desk. She sighed in relief at the momentary reprieve.

"You're pregnant, aren't you?"

"Ahh!" She jumped, screamed and twisted all at the same time.

Rick leaned against the wall to the left of the bathroom, arms crossed over his chest. She'd walked right past him without seeing him. Was he standing guard in case she needed him, or so she couldn't escape?

"My God, you scared me." She pressed a hand to her racing heart. She ignored his question for the moment. Damn him for being so astute.

She hadn't planned to tell him, but she wouldn't lie to him either.

"This isn't the first time you've been sick in the last couple of weeks. You're pale as fine porcelain, you've lost weight and you're constantly tired. All symptoms of pregnancy. And now you want to leave Sullivans'." He dropped his arms and straightened away from the wall. "Talk to me, Savannah."

She shrugged helplessly. "I don't know what to say, or how to explain—"

"I don't need explanations." He cut her off. "I know how babies are made and we took a few chances. What I need is confirmation. Are you pregnant?"

She slowly nodded.

His corresponding nod was much sharper. "We'll get married then."

Savannah swallowed hard. She'd expected the proposal, yet it still touched her, as did his acceptance of his participation in their circumstances. Some men would be looking to place blame or find a way out of the situation.

Tears welled up and a warmth grew ever bigger in her chest, spreading from her heart outward.

Oh, no. Oh, Lord. She loved him. In that moment she realized she'd been deluding herself. She'd thought knowledge would protect her, that making love to him with her eyes open and her expectations curtailed would prevent her from losing her heart to him.

Wrong.

The heart couldn't be controlled. Wouldn't be dictated to.

She went to him and, wrapping her arms around him, held him tight. His arms enveloped her, and where her head rested on his chest she heard his heartbeat accelerate. The instant chemistry almost convinced her to change her mind. How simple it would be to accept his proposal; she'd have great sex and financial security, and she'd inherit a whole family. All important factors, but not enough.

She wouldn't give up on her dream of love.

"Thank you." She stepped back and wiped at a stray tear. "But that's not necessary."

"It is, actually," he said, no give in his words or his stance. "My baby, my responsibility."

He couldn't have said anything more designed to put her back up. Or to tell her she'd made the right decision.

"No," she said, equally firm. "You've made it clear you have no intention of getting married or of having kids. I respect that and I'm prepared to raise this child alone."

"My decision not to marry or have children was a choice I made. Now the choice is gone. I'll do my duty." He went to his desk and began flipping through his calendar.

"We should get married as soon as possible. If we go with a civil ceremony, we could get it done by the end of the week." The look on her face must have warned him how off he was because he closed the calendar. "I suppose you want a church wedding with all the trimmings?"

"Yes." She crossed her arms over her chest. "When I get married that's what I'll want. But we're not getting married and rushing me isn't going to change my mind."

"I want to do right by you, by the child."

"If you want to be a part of your child's life, I'm not going to stop you, but it won't be as my husband."

"This is about your dad, isn't it?"

"This is about *me,* and the fact I deserve a partner who loves me, someone who wants to be with me for myself and not just because it's convenient or because duty demands it."

"That's nice, but you have a child to think of now."

"The best thing I can do for my child is put him or her in a loving, nurturing environment. *Duty* can't provide that. And I can't put myself in that situation again. I don't think my self-esteem could survive it."

He stepped close, tenderly pushing her hair behind her ear in a simple caress. "It doesn't have to be that way. I care about you. It won't be like it was with your dad. I've already started to delegate and give more authority to my managers. I didn't plan to have a child, but now one is here, I'll do whatever it takes to be a good father."

"I'm sure you'd try. And I appreciate that you want to." She backed away, creating necessary distance between them. "But I can't take the chance. The child and I will both be better off if you're a visitor in our lives. Then we won't expect too much from you."

"Don't you think you should give yourself time to consider my offer, to make sure you're making the right decision?"

He just didn't get it. "Can you say you love me?"

Silence greeted her question.

"Then I'm making the right decision. But you made the offer so your duty is met. Consider yourself off the hook." Holding herself tightly, she turned and walked to the door.

"Savannah." He stopped her before she cleared the entrance. "You *were* going to tell me, right?"

She bit her lip as she faced him. "Eventually," she admitted and then backed out the door.

CHAPTER NINE

SHORTLY before five, the door to Rick's office opened and his brother Rett entered. Rick waved him in while he listened to the vendor on the other end of the phone make excuses for an error in accounting.

Rett dropped into a visitor's chair facing the desk and crossed one leg over the other. Today he wore a navy so midnight-dark only the sheen showed blue. The gold of his St. Christopher medal gleamed in the open neck of his shirt.

Rick wrapped up the call after gaining a promise of reimbursement. He leaned back and met his brother's identical blue eyes. "Hey."

Rett grinned. "Congratulations, Daddy."

Unable to sit still, Rick rose to get a bottle of water from his mini refrigerator. "Thanks."

"What's wrong?" Rett waved off an offer of a drink, making no effort to hide his interest. "You're going to be a dad. You should be off-the-hook happy."

"Yeah, not so much." Rick scowled, still upset by Savannah's refusal to marry him. She talked about letting him off the hook, but that wasn't who he was.

Rett's raised brows reflected his puzzlement. "Trouble in paradise already? After your call I thought we'd be celebrating."

"No paradise. I proposed. She turned me down." Using succinct sentences, Rick explained the situation.

Rett contemplated Rick over steepled fingers pressed against compressed lips. After a tense study, Rett shook his head. "You need to woo her. It should be easy enough—you spend all day together."

"Not anymore. She quit. She took a job as a department assistant at a school. And I don't know when I'll have time to woo her. She's decided she wants to teach so she's going back to school."

"You're joking."

"Do I look like I'm joking?"

Rett lifted a dark brow. "You look constipated."

Startled by the off comment, a chuckle started low in Rick's throat, erupting in a full-body laugh. He threw back his head and enjoyed the freeing moment. Count on Rett to give it to him straight.

Drawing in a deep breath, Rick released the air along with a wealth of tension. He'd needed a serious reality check, and Rett hadn't hesitated to give it to him. Thank God for his twin.

"When you're right, you're right. Rett, I can't just let her go."

"You let Diana walk away, and you loved her," his twin pointed out.

The memory of that time had always had the

ability to upset Rick. But the pain of that loss paled in comparison to having Savannah deny him a permanent place in his child's life.

"That was fifteen years ago. I was young and an idealist. This is different. Savannah is expecting my child. I'm just going to have to change her mind."

"Good luck with that." Amusement gleamed unrepentantly in Rett's direct gaze. "I hope it happens soon. I wouldn't want to be you if Gram hears you're going to be a father and there's no engagement."

"I'm driving out to see her tomorrow. Maybe it won't be so bad. She's been after me to meet a nice woman and start a family."

"Yeah. I don't think this is quite what she had in mind." Rett laughed.

Rick pulled in to the long drive of his grandmother's Victorian home in Paradise Pines. The large white house still felt like home because of the woman who'd given up so much to help raise him and his brothers. Gram deserved to hear the news in person. He was going to be a father. The concept still rocked him to the core.

Him, a father.

Funny, the thought didn't freak him out as much as he'd expected, considering he'd given up all expectation of ever having a family of his own. He should be upset. Instead, he was having a hard time suppressing a rising excitement.

It didn't make breaking the news to Gram any easier, not when she'd sent Savannah to him. That would not sit well with her. Nor would Savannah's refusal to marry him, because he and his brothers had been raised to take responsibility for their actions.

No surprise, she took the first part of his announcement really well.

"You're going to be a father?" Joy lit up

Gram's aged features as she rose from her floral sofa to give him a hug.

He stood to return the embrace and she tugged him over to join her on the sofa.

"Tell me everything. I'd almost given up hope of you finding a nice young woman to change your mind from the lonely future you had planned for yourself."

Now came the hard part.

"You know her actually. The mother is Savannah Jones."

"I had a feeling about her." Gram clapped her hands. "Such a sweet child but with a lively spirit."

Yeah, that was Savannah. "Hardly a child or we wouldn't be in this situation."

"*Situation?*" A stern expression replaced the excitement on her face. "Derrick Francis Sullivan, you *are* going to marry this girl, aren't you?"

He cringed at the use of his full name, not

only because he hated it, but because she only used it in moments of extreme upset. Not that he didn't agree with her. Savannah's refusal to marry him still stung.

"I placed that woman in your care," she stated with regal dignity. "I cannot believe you'd take advantage of her, get her with child and not marry her. Explain yourself."

"Of course I asked her to marry me. She turned me down."

"Hmm." Gram gave him her I-know-you look. "Are you sure you *asked* her and it wasn't just a statement of intent?"

Feeling his cheeks heat guiltily, he scowled. "What difference does it make? I'm willing to marry her—isn't that enough?"

"Well, with that kind of enthusiasm I don't know how the girl could turn you down."

"We have a child to consider. We don't get to just think of ourselves."

She inclined her curly gray head. "What reason did she give for turning you down?"

"She said she wants to marry for love, and that she doesn't want a husband who's a workaholic like her dad."

"Ah." Gram nodded while compassion came into the blue eyes she'd passed on to her grandsons. "I don't know the whole history there, but Savannah practically raised her younger brother and sister. And she was barely more than a child herself."

"He skipped out on them emotionally after her mom was diagnosed with cancer. Sank into his work and never really came back out."

Gram tsked. "It must have been very hard on her."

"Right. She should marry me so I can make it easier for her this time."

"I don't know." Gram settled back in her corner of the sofa and eyed him seriously. "Maybe she's right."

Outraged, he shot to his feet. "How can you say that? I'm *nothing* like her father."

"Savannah is your assistant, Rick," Gram reminded him. "I think she knows your work habits. Which were fine when you didn't intend to marry, as you often said you wouldn't. But those habits are hard to break."

"Taking care of the company *is* me providing for my family."

"A woman needs more than a paycheck in a partner," she pointed out.

"Of course I know that." He paced the floral area rug he'd crawled on as a baby. "I can cut back on my hours."

"It'll take more than a change in schedule." His grandmother folded her hands in her lap. "It'll take a change in mind-set. I've tried to talk to you about your father before, but you weren't willing to listen."

No, he didn't want to hear. What was the point of hearing the details of failure?

"He ran the company into the ground," he stated grimly. "That's all I need to know."

"Life is rarely so simple. You should have learned that by now. You think of your father as weak because he chose to spend his time with his family over the business."

"He had a duty to provide for us. Dad was your son. I understand you don't want to hear anything bad about him, but what would we have done if the company had gone bankrupt?"

"It wouldn't have gotten to that point." Gram patted the sofa beside her. "Come sit with me. Let me tell you how it was."

"Gram—"

"Sit!"

Rick sat and hung his hands between his knees. He'd listen, but it wasn't going to change anything.

"Did you know your mother once left your father?" she asked.

"What?" Startled, he turned his head and nailed his grandmother with a glare. "No way."

"Oh, she did." Gram nodded emphatically. "Business was never in your father's heart. He preferred archaeology. He actually met your mother on a dig. They settled down when you kids started to come along, though they stole away to a dig every year or so. But they went through a bad patch after you and Rett were born. Your grandfather passed away that year and your dad stepped up to run the store. You two were a lot to handle, but your dad had to put in a lot of time to run the business."

Rick shook his head. He'd never heard any of this.

Gram placed a hand on his thigh. "Just listen. When your mom got pregnant with Ford she told your father he needed to help out more at home or she was leaving. He promised he would, and I believe he had good intentions."

Rick's grandmother stopped to reach for a

tissue from the box on the coffee table. Her hand trembled, and he realized how hard this was for her.

"Gram," he said painfully.

"I'm fine." She waved off his concern. "And you need to hear this." She drew in a steadying breath. "Your dad didn't make enough of a change, so your mom packed you kids up and went home to her parents. It killed your dad to be without his family. Eventually he convinced her he'd change. And he did. It took a while for the toll to show at the store, and when it did, he hired a manager. But by then we were in the middle of a recession, and then shortly afterward your parents were gone. It was my decision to let the manager go and run the store myself, which probably wasn't fair to you boys."

"Stop," he demanded, unwilling to listen to her speak ill of herself when he remembered how hard she'd worked to hold home and store together. "You did the best you could."

Her blue eyes teared up as she nodded. "That's what I'm trying to tell you. We can only ever do our best. Sometimes it pays off. Sometimes you have to adjust and try again. Your father changed because he had a lot to lose. Promising to change and not really making an effort hurts everyone involved. So be careful what you promise."

CHAPTER TEN

Two months later Rick sat in a doctor's office with Savannah and watched the screen as the doctor moved a ball in jelly across Savannah's abdomen.

"See, here's the baby's head and the feet. And here—" the doctor, a white-haired man with wire-rimmed glasses, pointed at a blip on the screen "—you can see the heart beat."

Rick squinted at the spot indicated and then he saw it, the pulsing beat of his child's heart. And yes, there was the head, and the arms and legs and the tiny feet.

"Rick, do you see?" Savannah fumbled for his hand.

"Yeah." Awe filled him to overflowing. Not taking his eyes from the small heartbeat, he wrapped his fingers around hers and squeezed. "Our baby. It's beautiful."

In an instant his world changed beyond anything he'd ever known. The sense of duty and responsibility increased a hundredfold, but added to that was an emotion so profound it filled his soul.

This was a love like nothing he'd ever known.

"No, not an *it* anymore." Savannah stared at the screen, turning her head this way and that to try and work out what she was seeing. "Dr. Wilcox, are we having a boy or a girl?"

Rick found himself holding his breath. Not that it mattered. Boy or girl, he just hoped for a healthy baby, knew Savannah felt the same.

"You are having a baby boy."

A son. For the first time ever he had an inkling of what his father must have felt. Was it possible to feel six times this much love? Rick couldn't imagine it.

"Ouch. Rick!" Savannah exclaimed.

He blinked at her and then looked down to

where he felt a yanking on his hand to find he was crushing her fingers in his.

"Oh, sorry." He immediately loosened his grip.

She grinned at him. "Pretty intense, huh, Daddy?"

"It's the biggest thing I've ever done."

"Me, too." The look in her green eyes softened and when she turned back to the monitor and tears welled, he understood exactly how she felt.

He leaned down to kiss her just behind her left ear.

She smiled and turned her hand in his to thread their fingers together.

"Marry me," he whispered. "Let's be a family."

She went totally still. When she came to life again she flicked him an unreadable look from the corner of her eye. A moment later she was focused on the screen again, even white teeth torturing her plump bottom lip.

But she just shook her head silently.

* * *

After the appointment Savannah sat at a traffic light tapping the steering wheel with nails painted in Pixie Dust Pink waiting for Claudia to answer her cell. Savannah's mind churned with thoughts of the doctor's appointment she'd just left. Of the second marriage proposal from Rick she'd turned down.

That did not get easier with practice.

"Hello." Claudia finally picked up.

"It's a boy," Savannah announced to the hands-free kit attached to the dash. She grinned and patted her bulge, a boy.

"A nephew! Woohoo!" Claudia whooped. "I knew it. I told Daniel you were having a boy. Have you told Rick?"

"I didn't have to. He was there. And yes, he's thrilled." Not that he'd made a big show of it, but she knew he was pleased.

Though, like her, he'd be happy whatever the gender as long as the baby was healthy. She always breathed easier after hearing the doctor say everything looked good.

"He showed up at your appointment again?"

"He wanted to drive me, but I have a meeting back at the school so I insisted on driving myself."

The fact Rick had been at all her appointments still surprised her. She saw almost as much of him now as she had when she'd worked for him. Especially during those last couple of months when he'd been avoiding her.

Who knew that by quitting she'd be freeing him to pursue her? On the days she didn't have her college classes, he'd stop by her home bringing dinner with him or charming—okay, bullying—her to go out with him. A few times she hadn't felt like going out, so she'd cooked.

She could tell he liked those times best, though he never expected it. And she realized that for all his bluster about staying single he was as much a family man at heart as any of his brothers.

No question she'd have more distance and privacy if she'd continued to work for him.

"Hey, I wanted to give you the news. Now I need to call and tell Daniel you were right. I'll see you on Saturday."

The light turned green, and Savannah pulled forward. The squeal of brakes gave her little warning. She looked up, saw an SUV barreling for her. Sheer instinct had her slamming both feet down on the brakes.

She screamed.

Claudia frantically called out her name.

And then everything went black.

Savannah lay in the hospital bed cradling the bulge that was her baby and fighting back tears. She was bleeding and the doctors were worried.

She was terrified. And alone.

She remembered talking to Claudia. Everything after the call blurred in a kaleidoscope of scary, painful events. The SUV had run a red light and hit the front of her sedan broadside. The police had told her if she hadn't stood on her brakes it would have hit her right in the driver's-side door.

She could be dead right now.

Gulping back a sob she rubbed her belly. Instead her baby might die.

"Sir, you can't go in there. You need to check in with admissions. *Sir!*"

A large, bronzed hand pushed the curtain aside and suddenly Rick was there. In the next instant he held her in his arms. He didn't lift her but came down to her. She wrapped her arms around him, hung on tight and let the tears flow.

"I'm here, Savannah," he crooned against her ear. "Everything is going to be fine."

Oh, he lied. But it was exactly what she needed to hear.

"The baby," she choked out.

"Our boy is strong," he assured her. "He'll

make it through this. How are you? Are you hurt? They wouldn't tell me anything."

"Shook up, a little bruised. The air bag saved me. But it was like a punch to the gut, and the baby…" She buried her face in his chest. "I'm bleeding. I'm so sorry."

"Stop. It's not your fault. None of this is your fault." He repeated it again and again until she almost believed it.

He stayed with her and eventually she calmed enough to tell him what she knew. A nurse came along to say the doctor had ordered an ultrasound and they'd be moving her in a few minutes.

Through the next hours she clung to Rick's hand. He stood by her side, his presence lending her strength, his touch giving her hope, especially when the doctors said they wanted to keep her and the baby under observation overnight and reevaluate the situation in the morning.

* * *

"Placental abruption is the separation of the placenta from the uterine lining," Doctor Wilcox stated the next afternoon. "I believe you have a partial separation caused by the trauma to the abdomen."

"That sounds serious." Heart beating frantically, Savannah squeezed Rick's hand.

"It is," the doctor confirmed. "The placenta is part of your baby's life-support system. When the placenta separates from your uterine lining, it can interrupt the transportation of oxygen and nutrients to your baby."

"Rick."

He circled her hand with both of his and held on tight. "Are you saying she's going to lose the baby?" he asked.

"She hasn't yet—that's a good sign. Plus his heartbeat is strong, which is an excellent indication of his chances. But you have to be cautious. I'm going to order complete bed rest for the next month and then we'll see. I want to monitor the baby carefully, at least once a week."

He went on to outline the limitations of bed rest and to caution her against overdoing things. She wondered how she was going to manage, especially when he mentioned she should have someone with her day and night.

A few minutes later Rett arrived and the doctor took his leave. Savannah tried to hold it together as family came and went through the evening, as the prognosis was repeated again and again.

Even her dad came by, which touched Savannah, but she was so emotionally overwrought she didn't know how to act. Rick saw the toll it was all taking on her and chased everyone on their way.

And then he held her while she cried herself to sleep.

"Are you ready to marry me now?" Rick asked from where he stood by the window.

Head bowed, she frowned down at the serviceable blue blanket covering her to the waist. Stupid, rough, ugly blanket.

"You're seriously taking advantage of a pregnant woman when she's down?" she exclaimed.

"I'll do whatever it takes." He crossed his arms over his chest, the gesture a wordless statement of his determination. "It's the practical solution to the situation."

Flicking him an irritated glance she said, "You might want to try something more romantic next time."

"Will that work?" Speculation lit up his eyes.

"No, but it'll mix it up for me."

Suddenly he was next to the bed, and she was framed by the magnificent columns of his muscular arms. And then his mouth was on hers, hard, hot, urgent, a demand and a declaration. When he lifted his head, resolve burned in his gorgeous blue eyes.

"Be warned. I'm not going to stop asking until I get the answer I want."

Savannah licked her lips as she stared up into all that heated intensity. Okay, what he lacked in romance, he definitely made up for in tenacity.

"You're not supposed to rile the sick lady. Just because I've been ordered to undergo bed rest doesn't mean I get to do anything interesting while I'm there." Turning sullen again, she plucked at the ugly blanket. "Over four months in bed. I'm going to go nuts."

Rick kissed her again, this time slow and sweet. "Don't get ahead of yourself. Take it one day at a time. Plus I know you. You'll find a way to fill the time."

"That'll be hard to do from a hospital room." The doctor had ordered complete bed rest for the first month with a possible move to moderate bed rest for the rest of her term, depending on how the baby was doing at the end of the first month.

The problem was complete bed rest meant no cooking, no chores, no moving around her apartment. If she didn't have someone to help her at home, they wanted to put her in a long-term facility. The thought of that made her want to cry.

But she wasn't willing to marry Rick just to keep from being bored. And she told him so.

"I have a proposition," he said, dropping into his customary chair beside the bed. "Come live with me. I talked to my housekeeper last night. She's willing to extend her hours and work from eight to four. That means you'll only be alone a couple of hours a day."

"Really?" It sounded perfect. Except it probably came with a ring attached. "Even though I'm not going to marry you?"

He lifted a dark brow. "My proposal stands. But, no, a marriage ceremony is not necessary for you to stay with me."

She eyed him suspiciously. "What's the catch?"

"You sleep with me."

Oh, no, not a good idea. "The doctor said no sex."

"Yeah, I was sitting here when he said it. This isn't about that. I'm not going to do anything to hurt the baby."

"Then why?" she asked.

"Because I won't be able to sleep at night worrying about you."

"Oh, come on." She just kept herself from snorting.

"I'm serious. What if you start having pains or fall while going to the bathroom? Anything could happen and I might not hear you if you call out. I need you where I can see you, hear you, reach out and touch you."

His intensity was back. Stronger, more stark. Yeah, he was serious. But could she do as he asked, sleep beside him every night for the next month, and probably more? Close enough to see, to hear, to touch.

What was the alternative? A sterile room with an antiseptic smell, and rough, ugly, blue blankets? And inevitable, eternal boredom? Sure, family and friends would call and visit, but there were so many hours in the day, and too many during the night. Usually a positive person, Savannah felt lonely just thinking about it.

Inside her a tiny movement stirred. She caught her breath and went completely still.

"What is it?" Concerned, Rick returned to her bedside and reached for her hand. "Are you in pain? Is it the baby?"

The flutter came again and she grinned through the tears blooming in her eyes. Pushing aside the blanket, she moved his hand to her belly, covered only by her thin nightshirt.

"It *is* the baby, but it's all good. He's moving." She pressed her hand over Rick's right where the tiny sensation stirred. "Do you feel him?"

He shook his head, and she saw that overwhelmed by emotion, words had failed him.

"I do. He's moving. He's going to be okay," she said and believed it. For the first time since the accident, she felt encouraged, the small movement of her child the medicine she needed to look forward again.

Rick sank into the chair and laid his head in her lap. She wished she could see his face but he was turned away from her. Threading her fingers through his chocolate-brown hair, she gave him a moment. When she felt her nightshirt grow slightly damp, she swallowed the lump in her throat and made a decision.

"Do you promise not to harass me about getting married?"

"I won't ask more than once a day."

She shook her head. Stubborn man.

"Okay. I'll come live with you."

* * *

Savannah moved in on Saturday. Rick saw it as a triumph. Now if only she looked happy about it.

With great satisfaction he got her settled in his bed and then propped his hands on his hips and surveyed her. A small frown puckering between her russet eyebrows, she looked around the room.

He followed her gaze, seeing his space through her eyes. His style ran to traditional comfort. A king-size black leather sleigh bed with a burnished nutmeg finish dominated the room with accompanying nightstands and bureau. Light flooded in through ceiling-to-floor multi-paneled windows, reflecting off the beige suede comforter and showcasing the brown-and-beige medallion rug. Lush green plants added color and a sense of luxury.

"Do you like it?" he asked.

"It's lovely." Nice words but they held no feeling.

She was depressed, and it wasn't because she'd officially started her bed rest. At least not entirely. Today was Claudia's graduation and Savannah was missing it.

He knew how much she'd been looking forward to this day, how proud she was of her sister. For that reason he had a surprise for her.

"Let me show you what I've got set up for you." He went to the closet and pulled out a hospital table, one of those that swung over the bed. On it sat her laptop computer. "Your link with the world."

"Rick." She fingered the laptop and forced a smile for him. "You're too good to me."

Wanting a real smile, he angled the computer toward him, hit a couple of keys to bring up the live stream from San Diego State, and then turned the screen back to her.

"What's this?" She blinked and focused on the video feed. She pulled the laptop closer. "Is that State?" Turning gleaming eyes up to him, she demanded, "Claudia's graduation?"

"I know how much you wanted to go. But you're doing everything you can to take care of our baby, so I got the IT department to show me how to set up the live feed and Daniel agreed to video it. I wanted to surprise you."

"You have." There was the genuine smile he sought. Beaming, she patted the bed beside her. "Come watch with me."

Nodding, he walked around the bed, climbed in next to her and leaned back against the black leather headboard to watch the ceremony.

"Once you see her get her diploma, you have to rest, because your family is coming back here after the ceremony."

"Really?" She turned hopeful eyes toward him. "They're coming here?"

"Straight from the graduation. Including your dad. Are you going to be okay with that? I don't want you getting upset."

"I was glad he came to the hospital. Too much of an emotional mess to show it, but I was really glad he came. And Daniel said Dad's been dropping by his place quite a bit recently, getting to know his granddaughter."

Tears welled in her eyes, but her smile never dimmed. It felt good to have her here, to know she and the baby were in his care. He was glad to give her this after all she'd been through.

"You can personally give Claudia her gift."

"Thanks to you." She snuggled closer to him. "This is the best surprise ever."

CHAPTER ELEVEN

SAVANNAH tied off the large black bow on the silver gift-wrapped package, pleased that it looked striking yet masculine. A week ago Jesse had mentioned today was Rick and Rett's birthday. Knowing Rick wouldn't go along with any fuss, Savannah had planned a surprise for him.

He'd given her several beautiful surprises so she owed him.

She grinned. It felt good to be in control of something again, nothing elaborate as she was still mostly stuck in bed and had to rely on others to do the work for her. But she had a plan and she was putting it into action.

With the package wrapped and the smell of baking chocolate cake drifting from the kitchen, she made a call to Rick's favorite Italian restaurant and ordered a meal of lasagna, salad and bread.

At three-thirty she showered and washed her hair, scrunching in mousse and leaving it to air-dry in long, loose curls while the housekeeper went through the closet to find her something besides sweatpants to wear.

"This is nice." Sybille showed her a black knit halter dress. Braided material criss-crossed the bodice before tying behind the neck and the hem fell all the way to the floor.

"Oh my. That must be one of the pieces Jesse picked up for me." Rick had insisted Savannah have some new comfortable clothes to celebrate the move to moderate bed rest. She'd protested because it turned out not to be that big a difference, which meant there was little motivation to get dressed in anything beyond sweats and pajamas.

But if this was a sample of what she now

owned, she might need to make an effort. And now she thought of it, Rick might enjoy seeing her in something more appealing than sweats.

"Thanks, Sybille. It's perfect."

"It'll look stunning with your pale skin and vivid hair." Sybille laid the dress on the end of the bed.

"You don't think it'll wash me out?"

"Not if you put a pop of color on your lips."

Savannah pawed through her cosmetic case and chose a tube of lipstick. She rolled it up for Sybille to see the deep bronze color.

The German woman shook her head. "Scarlet, to bring out the red in your hair."

Frowning down at the contents of her case, Savannah chewed her bottom lip. "I don't think I have anything like that."

"I do." Lushly round and eternally blonde, though easily in her fifties, Sybille hurried out and came back a few minutes later with her purse in hand. But she held back. "Would you allow me to redo your makeup?"

Savannah hesitated for just a moment and then nodded. What the heck? Sybille obviously knew makeup secrets. She always looked great even though she came to cook, clean and to keep Savannah company. She suspected the woman had a bit of the cougar in her.

With a glint in her eyes that made Savannah nervous, the older woman placed the mirror out of Savannah's reach and then suggested she change first. A few minutes later Sybille sat beside her on the bed and reached into the cosmetic bag.

"The cake is iced and ready," Sybille said as she wielded a shadow brush over Savannah's eyelids. "Do you want me to set up a table in here?"

"No. I was thinking the living room. Can you organize two place settings on the coffee table?

The food should arrive just after he gets home, and everything will be ready."

"He's going to be very surprised."

"Happily, I hope."

"Open." Sybille held up the lipstick, then applied it when Savannah complied. "Ah, yes. When he sees you, he will be happy."

Taking the proffered mirror, Savannah sighed at her reflection. The colors were subtle, her creamy skin softly highlighted with a warm blusher and the pop of scarlet on her lips was actually more of a lush dark cherry. "Sybille, you've made me beautiful."

"The beauty was already there. I just brought it to the surface."

"Thank you. For everything."

"It is my pleasure. Now, what more can I do?"

"That's it. Once the table is set, I just need five o'clock to roll around for Rick to get home."

But instead of greeting Rick at five, she got a phone call that he'd be an hour late as Rett wanted to go for a beer. He didn't mention it was their birthday but she understood, so she assured him she'd be fine for another hour.

She wasn't so fine an hour and a half later when the door opened and it was Sybille returning with the message Rick had been detained even further.

Savannah tried to fight the resulting depression. After all he hadn't known she'd planned a surprise. But the scene was too familiar, the disappointment too sharp for her to be gracious.

Why wasn't she important enough to come first once in a while?

He hadn't even called her himself, but had rung the housekeeper to come babysit. Could the message be any clearer?

"I'm so sorry, Savannah." Sybille sat on the couch and gave her a hug. "I know how important this was to you."

"I'm fine." Savannah pasted on a smile. No reason to bring Sybille down with her. "Good idea, bad timing. Can you freeze the lasagna? I'm not really very hungry."

"I was going to tell him—"

"No," Savannah said, a little too loudly. How mortifying would that be? "Let him enjoy his dinner with his brothers. We'll have our cake tomorrow."

"Okay. Except you have to eat. Let me heat some of this up for you."

The thought made her ill. "I don't think I can."

"Some soup then, or a salad. What would you like?"

"Whatever's easy. I'm going to go change."

"Oh, not yet. You look so pretty. Let me enjoy my handiwork a little longer." At her reluctant nod, Sybille smiled. "Lovely. Now I'll go make our dinner."

Laughter broke out as Ford, Rick's youngest brother and a navy SEAL, ribbed Rett over his fashion sense.

"You're just jealous because I don't have to wear a uniform," Rett shot back.

Rick looked at the faces of his brothers grouped around the table. They'd all come out to surprise him and Rett. And it was fun. But all he'd really wanted for his birthday was a quiet night at home with Savannah.

He'd gotten used to having her around. For all he hadn't planned to marry, he'd learned a bit about what he'd chosen to give up: the companionship, the laughter, the support and concern for his happiness. She made it all so easy.

And that's what he wanted tonight.

"Sorry, guys." He stood up. "Thanks for coming out. I love you all, but I'm going to go home."

"What?" Rett demanded. "I thought you were staying for dinner?"

"I was, but Savannah is at home alone. She's stuck there every day. It doesn't feel right to be out having a good time without her."

"But you already made arrangements to stay."

Rick shrugged. "Then it'll be a surprise when I show up."

"A surprise? Cool." Ford knocked knuckles with Cole. "Let's go. We can call our ladies and have them meet us at your place."

"No." Rick threw a credit card on the table. "Stay and enjoy dinner. My treat. I'll see you all at Sunday dinner." With a sense of deep satisfaction, he turned and headed home.

A short drive later he opened the door to find Savannah, sexy in wild curls and a hot black number, sitting on the couch. On the table were place settings for two and a huge chocolate cake.

"Oh man. On sh—" Rick bit off the curse. He watched her duck her head, but not before he saw the sheen of her tears.

His heart sank. "I'm so sorry."

Obviously she'd meant to surprise him. And he'd ruined it by staying out with the boys. He cringed inside, remembering how she'd told him she'd stopped believing in surprises because it hurt too much when they didn't come off as planned.

"I thought you were having dinner with your brothers," she said to the hands in her lap.

"I couldn't stay." He lifted her chin to look into her flooded green eyes. "I wanted to spend my birthday with you."

"Really?" she whispered.

"Yes. And I'm glad I did. You look amazing." He leaned in to nibble her ear. "Good enough to eat."

That earned him a small smile. "There's lasagna from San Fillipio's."

"I'm sorry I wasn't here for your surprise."

Her gaze was back on her hands. "You called a ba-a-bysitter for me."

He flinched at the catch in her voice and the pain it revealed.

"That was thoughtless of me," he admitted.

"I just didn't want you to be alone. And then I realized what I really wanted was to come home to you."

She leaned her head on his shoulder, and he felt her relax against him. "I'm glad."

Relieved at her acceptance, he stole a quick kiss.

"I hope there's plenty of cake, because I have a feeling the surprises aren't over yet. I tried to dissuade my brothers from following me home when I left early, but my guess is they'll be here shortly," he said wryly.

She cupped his cheek. "They love you and want to spend time with you. How could I object to that?"

A particularly rambunctious kick woke Savannah from a sound sleep. She smiled in the dark, pleased by Derrick Charles's hearty kick. Or Adam Joseph's, depending on who won the name game. She and Rick were still negotiating. Charles was to honor Rick's grandfather, as was Joseph. But she'd liked Derrick as soon as she heard it was Rick's full name.

Who knew? And Rett's full name was Everett. He was so *not* an Everett, which showed how important a name was.

She rubbed her bulge, pleased by the baby's vigorous activity, evidence of his continued growth.

Rick rolled over, his warmth blanketing her back as he cradled her to him, his hand coming to rest on her belly next to hers. He'd been on the phone with England when she went to sleep. They were having trouble with the installation of the new vault. She'd missed him. In the past couple of months she'd come to relish the nights when she got to languish in his arms.

"Adam is active tonight," he murmured.

"You mean *Derrick* is active tonight."

She felt him smile against her hair.

"The doctor is pleased with his progress. He's

well within the growth rate for this point in your term."

"Yes, I was excited by his optimism today."

Rick kissed her behind the ear. "You're not disappointed to continue the bed rest? I know you were hoping for a little freedom."

"Some, but the baby's growth is more important. If Dr. Wilcox believes it'll make a difference, I'm not going to argue."

"Has it been that bad?" The total lack of emotion in his voice spoke volumes.

Needing to see him, Savannah slowly rolled over to face him and he gently helped her get resituated by arranging the pillows that helped support her.

"Not at night, not when I'm with you," she assured him and he relaxed. She traced the dark shadow of his jaw, visible because of the light he insisted on leaving on in the bathroom.

"But the days are so long. Jesse has been a lifesaver. She drafted me to help with Gram's party. She brings Troy and sometimes Allie and comes over almost every day with something for me to take care of or just to talk over the status of everything. I know that she could handle it all alone, but still the work and the company have helped to keep me sane."

"What about your online classes? I thought those were keeping you occupied?"

She loved her classes, loved the sense of accomplishment they gave her. Pursuing a degree in education gave her a whole new sense of self-worth. She couldn't learn fast enough.

"They do. And I shouldn't complain because I have such great support from my family and from your family. I'm not lonely, just antsy. And I should stop whining."

"You're allowed." He brought her hand to his mouth and kissed her palm. "Better to vent than to let the feelings fester. I can take it and the stress wouldn't be good for you or Adam."

"How can you be so good to me when I look like a beached whale?"

"You couldn't be anything but beautiful if you tried."

She smiled. "Ahh, and they say Rett is supposed to be the charming twin."

"It's not charm when it's true."

"Oh, Rick, you leave me breathless." Literally. The lack of flattery only made the rare compliments more poignant.

"Does that mean you're ready to marry me?"

Yes. The word almost sprang off her tongue. Every time he asked it got harder to say no.

He took such exquisite care of her. Every night he arrived home by five-thirty and promptly came in to see how her day had gone and to share the events in his before hitting the kitchen to heat up whatever meal Sybille had made for them.

Not once had he lost his patience with her, not even when she got snappy with him out of boredom, fear or just from whacked-out hormones. And he made the bedroom as much his prison as hers even when he didn't have to, spending most of his time either beside her in bed reading or watching TV or at the desk he'd set up in the corner so he could keep her company while he worked.

And no matter how big she got, he made her feel wanted.

He was constantly touching her, never missing an opportunity to hold her or kiss her, yet he always kept a tight rein on his desire, never allowing them to get too carried away. She'd offered to please him in ways that wouldn't hurt the baby, but he'd refused to take a chance by overstimulating her.

"No fair," she whispered, "you already asked today."

"That was technically yesterday. I'm just asking early today."

"Too early. My defenses are down."

"Good." He settled his lips on hers, taking her mouth in a slow and tender seduction that made her sigh, made her yearn. "Say yes."

"Oh, you do tempt me."

"Then take a chance," he urged and she heard the tension in his voice when he usually restrained himself from pushing.

"I can't." Because she loved him, and no one knew better than her how much it hurt when you loved someone more than they loved you.

Yes, Rick had surprised her by supporting her, by being physically present and an emotional rock. But it would be a huge error to mistake support for love.

"You've spoiled me so, it's already going to hurt to leave."

"So don't leave."

Could she stay? Could she give them a chance? Not counting the whole bed-rest thing and fearing for her baby's health, the past two months had been nearly perfect. Although she turned him down daily, she felt as though she was part of a couple.

Yet she couldn't forget the pain of living with a workaholic. The highs and lows, the disappointments, the loss of hope, of self, took over your life no matter how hard you tried to disassociate it from everything else. She didn't like who she became then—impatient, moody, needy. It wasn't a good place to be.

Not even for Rick would she go back there. Her son—their son—deserved better from his mother than watching her become a shadow to his father.

"I've been thinking like a dad." He rolled to his back, propped his head on his hands and spoke to the ceiling. "Delegating more, cutting back my hours. I've tried to be here for you. Haven't I proved how important you and the baby are to me?"

She longed to tell him she loved him, yet feared doing so. He had to say it first and through his own initiative. And then she wasn't sure she'd actually believe him. Hadn't he said he'd do anything to get her to marry him?

"I see the effort you're making." She plucked at the sheet between them. "But it's only been a couple of months."

He pinned her with a hard gaze, his eyes navy in the darkened room. "I'm not your father, Savannah. Don't punish me for his sins."

"I'm trying not to. But my father's shadow isn't the only problem. There's your father's ghost haunting us, as well."

"What do you mean?" he demanded.

"I'm sure you loved your father, but you also resent him. It sounds like he valued his time with his family above everything, yet you blame him for nearly destroying Sullivans'. I don't know if you can put family first, and I need to know you will."

"Taking care of the business *is* taking care of my family," he insisted.

"Sometimes." She'd give him that.

"Most of the time."

"The question is, will you know when it's not?"

He had no answer for that, and, for the first time since she'd moved in with him, they went to sleep without touching.

"This is such a lovely party. I love the mix of casual seating along with the banquet and cocktail tables. It invites people to mix and mingle between trips to the dance floor."

Stunning in a silver evening suit with an asymmetrical collar and long skirt, Mrs. Sullivan regally lowered herself into the opposite corner of the couch from Savannah.

"I understand you helped with a lot of the arrangements." She patted Savannah's hand where it rested between them on the leather cushion. "Thank you."

"Jesse did most of the work." Savannah gave

credit where it was due. "Really, it was a blessing to have something to keep me occupied. And the idea for the couches and chairs is courtesy of Rick. He insisted I have a comfortable place to sit all night, and I didn't want to be the only one, so I created the mix. It seems to be working out well."

"It's wonderful. My feet thank you. And Rick. Careful, dear." She caught Savannah in the middle of a yawn. "I have strict instructions to notify Rick immediately if you show signs of weariness or fatigue."

"Oh…your hair is lovely in that sleek French knot." Savannah sought to distract Mrs. Sullivan with a compliment. She was too excited at being a part of the music and revelry of the matriarch's grand party to leave so early.

She glanced to Rick, who stood surrounded by his brothers at the bar. With a wink at Savannah, Rett and the others had dragged Rick away. As she watched, they all laughed while Rett pretended to be stabbed in the heart. It made her happy to see Rick happy.

No, she wasn't ready to make an exit just yet, so she continued to praise her friend. "You're truly the queen of the ball tonight."

Mrs. Sullivan shook a finger at Savannah. "Flattery will not save you. I value my life and that of my great-grandson too much to thwart Rick."

"Oh, please don't tell him, Mrs. Sullivan," Savannah begged. "He'll banish me upstairs, and I'm having too much fun. And it wasn't flattery—you look so sophisticated and vibrant you glow tonight. And way too young to be celebrating your eighty-fifth birthday."

"Bless you, child, the secret is in the dim lighting, a good girdle and a really expensive face powder. But a woman does what she must when she's the star of the show."

Savannah laughed and patted her prominent

belly. "There's no tucking this guy out of sight. He likes the music. He's been dancing all night."

Delighted, Mrs. Sullivan put out her hand. "May I?"

"Of course." Savannah held the older woman's hand over the baby's movements.

"You need to call me Gram." Tears welled in Mrs. Sullivan's vivid blue eyes when the baby bucked against their fingers. "You are family now. Because of this little guy. But even more for the happiness I see in my grandson's eyes. Thank you for bringing him back to us."

Gram placed her other hand over Savannah's and squeezed her fingers. "That's better than any birthday present anyone could ever give me."

"You're welcome. But Rick hasn't really gone anywhere."

"Dear, he's been distancing himself a little bit at a time for years. Making it to fewer Sunday dinners or just making an appearance at bigger events."

"Always too busy?" Savannah bit her lower lip. This was exactly the behavior she feared from Rick. But now she was hearing about it, surprisingly, it didn't feel right.

"That was his excuse, yes. But that changed after your trip to England. I was very excited when he had the family to his place for Sunday dinner. That was a first and it was all because of you."

"He's always looking for ways to keep me entertained," Savannah confirmed.

"It's more than that. He's made it clear to everyone in the family that you're his wife whether you decide to make it official or not. I'm hoping you will. I've been dodging Father John all night."

"Mrs. Sullivan!" Savannah giggled.

"Gram," the older woman insisted.

"Gram." Savannah's throat tightened on the

word. This family's generous welcome touched her deeply. Rick's grandmother deserved to know the truth. "You shouldn't get your hopes up. Rick has been wonderful, but this child, me, we're only a duty to him. He'd treat anyone in his care the same way."

"You're too smart not to see how he feels about you. You're just afraid to believe it."

"You think I'm smart?"

"Of course, especially at reading people. I wouldn't have recommended you to Rick as an assistant otherwise. You're too close to this situation if you can't see that he loves you."

Hope bloomed in her heart at Gram's declaration, but she quickly squashed the feeling. Better not to delude herself.

"I think you're mistaking concern for something more," she said.

"And I think you're letting fear color your judgment. He's calmer, more contented than I've ever seen him. And you've brought laughter back into his life. I can see his effect on you, as well. You two belong together."

Savannah blinked back tears. "I wish I could believe that. But I can't afford to spin dreams out of hopes. I lived that way for years and all I got in return was indifference and disappointments. I can't do that to myself again. And I won't do it to my child."

Avoiding Gram's gaze, Savannah pleated folds into the skirt of her navy dress. "Rick has been married to the business too long to change now. With the baby at threat his strong sense of duty and responsibility are motivating his actions. When the baby gets here, he'll start putting in more time at the office again. And it's okay, because that's what makes him happy. But I need more from the man I marry."

"Oh, child, you're wrong. I wonder how long he has to prove himself to you before you believe in him. A year? Five years? How fair is that? Rick deserves a chance to make his own mistakes, not his father's or your father's."

Stricken by this stark truth, Savannah watched Gram stand and smooth down her skirts.

"I'm fond of you, Savannah. You survived a tough childhood. And there's no denying you're right—you deserve a man who loves and adores you. But I'm going to leave you with one thought. The only thing worse than the lack of trust in a relationship is the lack of faith."

CHAPTER TWELVE

SUNDAY morning Rick zipped his suitcase and lifted it to the floor. His flight to London left in two hours. Rett would be here in a few minutes to drive him to the airport.

He didn't want to go, didn't want to leave Savannah, but the security issues with the vault needed to be addressed. With no one on-site to oversee the work, the renovations were moving too slowly. Rick planned to hire a manager while he was in the area.

Looking up, he met Savannah's gaze from where she was propped up on the bed watching him. She wore white shorts and a pink tank top that matched the color on her toes. But her complexion was wan, the skin around her eyes drawn tight in fatigue from a restless night.

"You look pale," he said with concern. "I let you overdo it at Gram's party."

"I had a ball. And I'm fine." She smiled and held out a hand to him. "I miss you already."

He sat and, cupping her face in his hand, swept his thumb over her cheek, tracing the shadow under her eye.

"Say the word and I'll send Rett in my place."

"Please, we both know you're chomping at the bit to get there and whip everyone into shape."

"Maybe," he allowed, because part of him did. The total businessman he used to be would demand it. That man would have been on a plane when the company installing the new vault had first called about the problem.

But he'd changed.

"You know it's true." She took his hand and laced their fingers together.

"I know I'll miss you," he admitted.

"Then maybe you'll hurry home—ahh." She flinched and caught her breath.

"What is it?" he demanded. "Are you okay?"

"Yeah." She rubbed her belly. "It's just your son the baseball player getting in some practice."

"That must be your son. My son plays football."

No, he wasn't just a businessman anymore. He was a family man, too. It amazed him how his priorities had changed. How something that affected the store had always been his first consideration when it came to making plans and decisions.

Not anymore.

Savannah and the baby came first. It was clear to him now that they always would. Which was exactly what she'd asked of him—to put her first.

He loved her.

The truth of his feelings hit him in a rush. It was so simple, so clear, so deep he wanted to shout it from the mountaintops.

He opened his mouth to tell her just as a pounding sounded at the door. Damn, he'd have to wait until he got back. Better to do that anyway, as he wouldn't be rushing off halfway across the world. He'd be able to hold her, kiss her and finally convince her to be his wife.

There was a knock on the bedroom door and then Claudia stuck her head inside. "Rett is here."

"Thanks," Rick said, and she retreated, giving them a chance to say goodbye.

"Kiss me before he takes you away."

"First," he said, reaching for the baby monitor on the night table, "don't forget to give Claudia the monitor while she's staying here with you. I want her to be able to hear you at all times. I'll tell Rett, for when he takes over on Tuesday night. I'll be back Friday."

She completely ignored his instructions but pinned him with a suspicious gaze.

"I notice you didn't come up with the baby

monitor idea before you insisted I sleep with you."

Caught.

He leaned over her and claimed her mouth in a lingering caress, dragging the kiss out as passion surged between them. Finally he lifted his head and met her desire-drenched eyes.

"I wanted you in my bed."

"But we couldn't do anything."

"Didn't matter."

She swallowed hard. "Oh."

He kissed her again, short and urgent.

"We have to talk when I get home."

"About what?" Her hand tightened on his.

He shook his head, stepped back and grabbed his suitcase. "When I get back." He needed to go while he still could. "Be good, and try not to have the baby while I'm gone."

"Claudia!" Savannah yelled for her sister and then went back to her breathing exercises. She'd

been having little aches and pains all morning, so, after Rick left with Rett, it didn't take
Savannah long to realize there was more to the
pains than a little discomfort.

"You called?" Claudia strolled into the room.

"Can you get my overnight bag and put a few
things in it for me?"

"Sure. I've heard they advise you to have it
ready early, just in case. I can do it after we
eat. I'm making chicken salad and there's some
mango, yogurt and sweet rolls. Something
should spark your appetite. I thought we'd eat
out on the back deck, if you think the chaise
will be comfortable enough."

Savannah blinked at her sister, realized the
misunderstanding and fought the urge to snap
back.

"No, no, no. No chicken salad. Not just in
case." She swung her feet over the side of the
bed. "Now!"

Fear, uncertainty, anticipation and a hundred

other emotions raked at her nerves, pulling her in a hundred directions. In, out, she continued her breathing; as long as she remained calm everything would be okay.

"I called Dr. Wilcox." She gasped at a sharp pain. "He's meeting us at the hospital."

"What?" Claudia's eyes popped wide. "Now? You're having the baby now?" She dropped the dish towel she'd carried into the room and dashed to the closet. "You called Rick, right? Luckily the plane won't have left yet. He can meet us at the hospital, too."

"I'm not calling Rick."

She wanted Rick, needed him by her side. Yet she couldn't call him. The glitch with the security in the vault was a big deal; if it couldn't be fixed soon, they wouldn't be able to complete the remodel in time for the planned opening. And Rick wouldn't meet his goal of making Sullivans' Jewels international during their centennial year.

She hadn't told him because she couldn't stand to see him choose the business over her. It would break her heart.

"His flight doesn't leave for forty-five minutes." Claudia stepped out of the closet carrying an overnight bag. "If you call now, you can still catch him before he gets on the plane."

Shaking her head, Savannah said, "It's best if he goes."

Claudia looked confused. "You're not going to tell Rick you're in labor?"

"No." Savannah swallowed back tears. "And I don't want you calling him either."

This was the way it had to be. She could have this baby on her own, but not if she were agonizing over Rick's absence.

"Savannah." Obviously sensing something was wrong Claudia spoke very gently. "He has a right to be here."

"I'm the one having this baby, and I said *no.*" Savannah didn't care that she was being unreasonable. She needed to do what was best for the baby. And right now that meant thinking of herself first.

Dr. Wilcox was waiting at the hospital. Savannah was admitted quickly and, after a brief exam, he ordered the nurse to prep her for a cesarean delivery. Then he left to get ready for the procedure.

Claudia agreed to go with Savannah into the delivery room and was led away to get suited up.

Momentarily alone, Savannah lay staring at the ceiling, thinking Rick's plane was probably taking off over San Diego as she waited to go into surgery. At least twenty times she'd looked for him or reached out a hand, expecting his to wrap around hers in a show of support. So many times these last few months he'd been her strength, her rock, holding her steady when her nerves became shredded, keeping her company when frustration shortened her temper.

Each time she reached for him and he wasn't there was a reminder of every time she'd reached for him over the past months and he *had* been. Not at the office, at a meeting or away on business. But here for her. In so many ways he'd demonstrated his commitment to her and their child, but she'd been too blind to see, too afraid to believe.

Oh, Lord, he was going to be so angry she hadn't called him.

He should be here. More, he'd want to be here.

Her insecurities had cost her big this time, but, worse, they'd robbed Rick of the opportunity to be at his son's birth.

Gram's words about trust and faith echoed in Savannah's head and a new fear enveloped her. What if he couldn't forgive her?

She could lose him and it would be all her fault.

The nurse would be back in a minute. Savannah glanced toward the door but only saw the curtain guarding her privacy. She needed to act now. Maybe his flight had been delayed. Hands shaking, she dialed his cell. She needed to tell him about the baby, needed to tell him how wrong she'd been.

His voice mail came on. Disappointment crashed through her. Too late. She swiped at tears and almost hung up, but he deserved to hear about the baby from her.

"Rick, oh, Rick, I'm so sorry. I should have called sooner, should have had faith in you, but I was stupid." The door opened, but Savannah rushed on, hoping the nurse would give her a few minutes to finish. "So stupid. I was afraid you'd leave me to do this alone. But that was my fear talking. In my heart I knew better. Know better. You are the best man I've ever known. I love you so much—"

The curtain was pushed back and Rick stood there.

She blinked at him, unable to believe her eyes.

"That better be me you're talking to." He stepped over, gently took the phone from her and set it on the bedside table.

"Rick." She threw herself into his arms. They instantly closed around her and tightened, giving her a sense of wholeness and strength. "Claudia called you. Thank God."

"It should have been you." She heard the hurt in his voice and cringed.

"I know." She pulled back and framed his precious face in her hands. "I'm sorry. You've been so patient with me, so giving and all I've done is doubt you and hold back. I love you."

She ran her fingers down his cheeks, but looked at his hair, his lips, his chin, anywhere but his eyes.

"I was afraid to tell you, because it would give you too much power over me. But love isn't something you can harness or control. Hiding my feelings only weakened me and diminished us." She smiled through her tears. "I know you don't love me—"

"But I do."

She blinked. "What?"

"I love you." The declaration was all the more powerful for its simplicity. "I wanted to tell you before I left but I ran out of time."

"You love me?" Hope and joy sent warmth flowing through her. "Really?"

"Savannah." Rick cradled her hand in his, brought it to his mouth and kissed her palm. "Claudia caught me at the airport, but I'd already exchanged my reservation on the plane with Rett. I kept remembering how pale you looked, how active the baby was and I couldn't leave you. I love you. I love our child. I want to live the rest of my life with you."

"So you forgive me?"

"Of course I do. We're together now, and that's

what matters." Still holding her hand he shifted so he stood beside the bed. "I'd go down on one knee, but I wouldn't be able to see you. Savannah Jones, I love you. Will you marry me?"

A contraction hit.

Her breath caught in her throat and she clamped down on his fingers. Before the contraction finished and she could accept his proposal, Rick went into panic mode, which was really interesting to see for the thirty seconds it lasted.

He turned white while his gaze darted wildly around the room as if he might find the doctor hiding in the corner. He barked out questions and concerns that she had no breath to respond to.

Finally he caught himself, inhaled and gathered his control.

"Stay right there. I'm going to find the nurse."

She nodded between panting breaths. Right. She'd stay right here.

The nurse returned without Rick, declaring he was being prepped to join Savannah in the birthing room. From that point on there was no opportunity to speak to him alone. She was too busy having their baby.

A few hours later Rick stood at Savannah's bedside, his arm draped over her pillow, their fingers linked near her shoulder, watching his grandmother cradle his son in her arms. It was a sight he'd thought he'd never see.

What a waste it would have been.

The room was packed with people, with more waiting in the lobby for their chance to admire the newest addition to the family.

Savannah pulled on his hand and he looked down. Exhausted but euphoric, she'd never been more beautiful to him. Bending, he kissed her gently.

"You are amazing." He praised her. "Thank you for my son."

"Charles Joseph after your grandfathers. Gram is pleased."

"Gram is ecstatic. Little Joey will be the apple of her eye." He didn't know how life could get any better, except maybe being alone with Savannah and his son.

"Yes," she said softly.

"Yes?"

She smiled into his eyes. "I love you. And yes, I'll marry you."

His heart melted. Finally.

Life had just gotten better.

* * * * *